CORGI CASE FILES

CASE OF THE

HOLIDAY HIJINKS

J.M. POOLE

CORGI CASE FILES

CASE OF THE

HOLIDAY HIJINKS

BOOK 3

J.M. POOLE

Secret Staircase Books

Case of the Holiday Hijinks
Published by Secret Staircase Books, an imprint of
Columbine Publishing Group, LLC
PO Box 416, Angel Fire, NM 87710

Book layout and design by Secret Staircase Books
Cover images by Yevgen Kachurin, Irisangel, Felipe de Barros

First Secret Staircase paperback edition: November 2020
First Secret Staircase e-book edition: November 2020

* * *

Publisher's Cataloging-in-Publication Data

Poole, J.M.
Case of the Holiday Hijinks / by J.M. Poole.
p. cm.
ISBN 978-1649140234 (paperback)
ISBN 978-1649140241 (e-book)

1. Zachary Anderson (Fictitious character)--Fiction. 2. Pomme
Valley, Oregon (fictitious location)—Fiction. 3. Amateur sleuth—
Fiction. 4. Pet detectives—Fiction. I. Title

Corgi Case Files Mystery Series : Book 3.
Poole, J.M., Corgi Case Files mysteries.

BISAC : FICTION / Mystery & Detective.

813/.54

For Giliane —

I am the world's luckiest guy to have you by my side! Here's to many more years together!

Acknowledgements

I'm very thankful to get this book in the hands of the readers before Christmas. I tried so very hard to get *Case of the Fleet-Footed Mummy* out by Halloween but, sadly, it didn't happen. This time, I made it!

There are several people that made this book possible. First off, my wife, Giliane. She puts up with my incessant babbling and questions about Pomme Valley all the time. We even have some serious disagreements with how the town is run, but thankfully, we're able to work them out. Once more I need to thank the members of my Posse. You guys & gals are the best support team any author could hope for! Thank you very much for all your work! Once more, my hat is off to Felipe de Barros, artist extraordinaire. This is the second cover he's done for me and I'd have to say that I couldn't be more pleased. Well done, Felipe!

Last — but certainly not the least — I want to thank you, the reader, for giving my book a shot when there are so many hundreds of thousands to choose from.

I hope you enjoy the story! Happy reading!

J.

True happiness is coming home to find a corgi waiting for you!!

ONE

I'm really not too comfortable with any of this."

"Zack, relax. She'll never know."

"But it feels like I'm trying to hide this from her."

"You are trying to hide this from her. Trust me, what Jillian doesn't know cannot hurt her. I'm certainly not going to tell her. Are you?"

It felt like I had a full-blown fever raging through my system. My face felt like it was on fire. What if someone saw the two of us in here? Let's face it. Jillian seems to know every single person in Pomme Valley. What if someone lets it slip to her that I was having lunch with her best friend? What would people say? Forget that. What would Jillian say?

"Would you relax?" Hannah teased. "You'd think that … wow. Why is your face so red? Are you feeling okay?"

"I'm just nervous," I admitted.

"Why? Because we're deliberately doing this behind Jillian's back?"

I nodded. "That about sums it up."

"Look, all I'm trying to do is help you pick out the perfect Christmas present for Jillian. I know her better than you and I've known her a lot longer."

"I know that, but it still feels wrong. I'm just not a big fan of sneaking around."

"You're a good man, Zack," Hannah told me, giving me a wistful smile. "You and Jillian are perfect for each other. I am so happy for the two of you."

I wasn't too sure what to say to that. If memory serves, Hannah was the friend of Jillian's who was in an abusive relationship, but refused to leave her husband. Maybe she was trying to maintain the appearance of a normal family because she was ashamed? I don't know. I do know that Jillian has tried—numerous times—to help Hannah out should she ever be willing to leave Dylan, her husband.

"Neither of us wants to take things too fast," I reminded her, as I side-stepped around any reference to anyone being in a happy relationship.

"And that's commendable," Hannah said. "Since this is the first Christmas that you two will be spending together, your first gift for her should be a meaningful one."

"Okay. So, what do I get her? What does she like?"

Hannah sat back in her chair. She was silent as she considered the question. While she was contemplating her reply, I decided to get a refill on my soda. We were having lunch at Wired Coffee & Café, a favorite hangout for coffee-addicts everywhere. The only reason I liked coming here was sitting in the corner. The tall, shiny machine with the nineteen-inch LCD display beckoned enticingly as I approached. It was a soda machine, but the kind where you get to choose what base soda you want and then add customized flavorings to it. For the record, I just tried adding raspberry to my Coke Zero. I've liked practically every combination that I have tried, and since I like raspberries, I figured the two would be a good mix.

Wrong.

So now I've chosen an orange/vanilla mix to add to my soda. I've always been a fan of orange creamsicles. One sip had me smiling. Oh, yeah. I'll have to remember that one. I headed back to the table and noticed Hannah was watching me approach. I truly did feel sorry for her. Jillian had mentioned that Hannah spent so little time at her home that she might as well have slept at her store. And, in case you didn't know, Hannah Bloom owns and operates Pomme Valley's one and only florist shop, The Apple Blossom. I could only wonder what type of abuse Hannah had been forced to take. Hopefully that dick of a husband wasn't physically abusing her. Jillian has never said and I've never asked. Maybe I should have.

"I just wish they'd release a home version of that soda machine," I mused as I sat back down in the booth. "That thing is awesome. I'd buy one without a second's notice."

Hannah smiled at me. "What flavor did you get?"

"Umm, I guess you could call it 'orangesicle Coke Zero'."

"Orangesicle soda? I was getting ready to make a face, but it actually sounds kinda good. Not the Coke Zero part, but an actual soda without the fake sugar."

I grinned. "You sound like Jillian."

"So what would you like to know about her?" Hannah

asked, taking a sip from her iced tea.

"What does she like?" I asked. "What does she hate?"

Hannah sat back in her chair and studied me. She looked at the notebook I had brought with me. She stifled a giggle.

"You really are a writer, aren't you?"

I shrugged. "Yep. Don't mind me. I'm going to be taking some extensive notes here and then lock 'em in my safe so I won't ever lose them."

Hannah laughed. "Smart man, Zack. Okay, let's see. How much do you know about her?"

"Only what she's told me. She was married once, but lost her husband to cancer."

"Michael. Yes, that was rough on her. It's taken her a long time to heal, Zack. Don't even think about breaking her heart."

"I wasn't planning on it," I assured her.

"Jillian has lived in Pomme Valley all her life," Hannah continued. "She's one of those people who knew from an early age that this is the town she wanted to call home. I've never heard her express any desire to live anyplace else."

I nodded. "I knew she grew up here. I always figured she stayed put due to family and friends."

"That's only part of the picture," Hannah told me. "Look, I'm telling you this so that you'll understand what the concept of home means to Jillian. This is where she's happy. This is where she belongs."

I nodded. Hannah pointed at my notebook.

"It's at this point you'll want to start taking some notes. Are you ready?"

I flipped open my notebook, took out my favorite mechanical pencil, and nodded my readiness. Hannah stared at my open notebook for a few moments. I heard her clear her throat, so I looked up and gave her an expectant look.

"What type of books do you write?" she suddenly asked.

I'm sure the color drained right out of my face. I had yet to confide in anyone about what I write, which, by the way, are romance novels of the steamier variety. Not smut, but serious romance stories. I hadn't even told Jillian. That day will come. I spent years living in Arizona without a single person knowing what genre I wrote in. I'd just as soon keep it that way, so I was going to have to be careful not to let anything slip.

"Ummm, I never really mentioned it. Why do you ask?"

Hannah smiled at me the way a cat would smile at a canary. My throat suddenly felt like it was on fire. I didn't like that face. She was acting like she knew something. I hastily gulped down my soda. I'm also sure my face was as red as a lobster.

"Because I want to see how long it'll take you to admit that you're Chastity Wadsworth."

My soda spewed everywhere. Thank goodness I wasn't facing Hannah at the time or else she'd be covered with sticky soda pop. Bystanders turned to regard me curiously.

"Well, that confirms that," Hannah said, between giggles. "I knew it, Zack. I just knew that you were Chastity Wadsworth."

"Would you stop saying that out loud?" I gasped. "How did you figure it out? Please tell me that you haven't told anyone else."

"Your secret is safe with me, Ms. Wadsworth," Hannah giggled.

It pleased me to see that she was blushing just as much as I was. I pulled several napkins out of the dispenser and tried to mop up the mess I had made. Leave it to me to have a huge mouthful of soda when someone determines my romance writer pseudonym and then confronts me with it.

"How did you put it together?" I asked, dumping a handful of the sodden napkins into the trash.

Hannah waited until I was back at the table.

"I'm a huge fan of your books," Hannah told me as she leaned forward. "I've read everything that you've published and had wondered what had happened to you when you didn't publish anything for a few months late last year. I figured out that's when your wife died, am I right?"

I sighed. "You're right."

"Then you started writing again, only it wasn't the same. I could tell that the fire you had, the passion that drove you, well, it was missing from your books."

"My critics called it my 'unique edge'," I told Hannah. "I can't write if I'm not happy. And in Phoenix, looking around my old house, and expecting to see Samantha come walking around the corner at any time, it hurt. I couldn't write there. I needed a change of scenery."

"And that's when you moved here!" Hannah finished for me. "That's when you started writing again! I could tell you had become happy. Your books reflected that."

"I am happy here," I admitted, giving her a sheepish grin as I did. "It's strange. I own two dogs, an award-winning winery, and have started dating when I thought I'd never love again. Never say never, Hannah."

"If I bring you some books, would you sign them for me?"

I felt the flush creeping back up my neck.

"I will if you keep my identity secret. Don't tell anyone, not even Jillian."

"You haven't told Jillian that you're a romance writer?" Hannah asked, clearly surprised.

I shook my head. "No. Not yet. I will, don't get me wrong, just not yet."

"I can't believe that she hasn't asked what kinds of books you write," Hannah commented.

"She has, on a couple of occasions," I admitted. "Thankfully something else always comes up and the subject is changed. I will say, though, that I'm running out of ways to deflect the question."

"And if she's not only heard of your books but read them, too, what then?" Hannah asked.

"Then I'm sure we'll both get a good laugh out of it," I answered. "Now, enough about me. Back to Jillian."

"Right. Now, what was I saying about her?"

"You mentioned that she has lived here her entire life and, from the sounds of things, will never want to move away. I'm just not sure how that is supposed to help me pick out a gift. What, should I go down to the local cemetery and pick out a nice plot to give her? That's kinda morbid, don't you think?"

It was Hannah's turn to choke on her drink. She slapped a hand over her mouth but it wasn't in time to prevent iced tea from dribbling down her face. I grinned and pulled a few more napkins from the dispenser. I also noticed that the dispenser was close to running out. I handed her a few and tried to keep the smile off my face. Thankfully Hannah returned the smile.

"I like you, Zack. You have a terrific sense of humor.

I've sure made a mess, haven't I?"

"Please," I scoffed. "You didn't even get it off the table. Mine shot all the way to the next table over."

"Continuing on," Hannah said, wiping her hands and her face with the brown napkin, "after Michael died Jillian was able to purchase one of PV's historic houses, the one that she's had her eye on since she was a little girl."

"She's told me this," I said. "She purchased Carnation Cottage. It's a nice house. I'm sure that place had one heckuva price tag."

"Michael was very wealthy, not to mention that he had taken out a large insurance policy. He was a lot like you, Zack. He was caring. He never wanted Jillian to have to worry about anything in the event that something happened to him."

"Cancer," I said, shaking my head. "It's a terrible way to go."

"The worst," Hannah agreed. "When Michael passed, Jillian became determined to help people with all the new-found wealth she had acquired. She's donated to the hospital, renovated much of the high school, and…"

"I'm surprised they haven't named anything after her," I interrupted. "If she's given that much to the hospital, or the school, don't they customarily rename something as a way of saying thanks?"

"Oh, they wanted to," Hannah said, giving me a smile. "The hospital wanted to rename their entire west wing after her. The high school wanted to change the name of its auditorium. To say that Jillian was less than enthused would've been an understatement. She forbade anyone from plastering her name onto anything."

"I wonder why," I mused to myself.

"She's a fairly private person. She likes to hang out, be with friends, and be with you," Hannah told me, "but she doesn't like the attention."

"What else does she like?" I asked as I went back to my notebook.

"Lasagna."

I started scribbling. "Who doesn't?"

"Vegetable lasagna."

"Oh. Ugh. She doesn't like the traditional meat variety?"

"Oh, that too, but her favorite is spinach lasagna."

My stomach churned at the thought. My parents had made a spinach lasagna for dinner one night when I was little. My stomach recoiled then just as much as it was doing now. Spinach didn't belong in pasta. I know some of you people enjoy it, but I'm not one of them.

"She loves Crystal Rose champagne."

I groaned again.

"Have you heard of it?" Hannah asked, surprised.

"Champagne? Of course. Can't stand the stuff."

"No, I'm sorry, not just any brand of champagne but Crystal Rose. Have you heard of it?"

"No. Is that bad?"

"It's four hundred a bottle."

"For a stupid bottle of bubbly? Who in their right mind would shell out that much money for a lousy bottle of...?"

"Zack?" Hannah interrupted, stopping me mid-rant.

"What?"

"It's Jillian's fa-vo-rite," she slowly repeated. "She loves it."

"Oh. Crap. It figures. Is it sold here in town?"

Hannah shook her head. "No. You have to purchase it online. Look on the bright side. It comes with free shipping."

"For four hundred a bottle it had better be drop shipped here by private helicopter."

"Continuing on," Hannah said, suppressing a smile, "she loves chai tea drinks, made with…"

"Soy," I interrupted, recalling the horrible drink that I had mistakenly bought a few months ago when Jillian and I had first stopped off to get a drink together. I shuddered.

"I'm not doing too well, am I?" Hannah asked as she studied my face.

"It's not helping so far. Keep going. There's gotta be something in there that I can get her."

"Her favorite flower is the carnation."

I nodded. I already knew this. In fact, I even knew which color was her favorite.

"Do you know which color to get her?"

I nodded and offered Hannah a smug smile.

"As a matter of fact, I do. If I'm looking to get her carnations solely based on color, then it'd be red. If I'm looking for the most aromatic, then it'd be white or yellow."

"You're good," Hannah observed. "If you ever need to get her flowers, come see me. I'll give you the friends and family discount. Now, as you may have guessed, she loves cookbooks. Even if they're in a different language, she'll still love them. Oh. Purple bling. If it's purple, and it sparkles, you can rest assured that Jillian will like it."

I was writing so fast that I was sure smoke was coming off the paper.

"She recently confessed to me that she absolutely loves corgis."

I grunted. "I don't have any plans on getting another dog, thank you very much."

Hannah suddenly laid her hand over mine to stop me

from writing. Startled, I looked up at her and saw that she had tears flowing down her cheeks. Confused, I looked down at my notes. I had just scribbled a side note that she likes corgis. That was it. What had happened?

"What's the matter?" I asked, concerned. "Is everything all right?"

"You said you don't have any plans on getting another corgi," Hannah sniffed.

I sighed. "Does that mean she really wants a puppy? Oh, man. That's not what I..."

"Zack, let me finish. You said that you don't have any plans on getting another corgi, remember?"

"Yeah, so?"

"You're already thinking ahead. That tells me that you can already envision the two of you starting a life together. That's so sweet!"

"Whoa, wait. Hold up. We were talking about dogs, that's it. No one was talking marriage."

Hannah pulled the last napkin from the dispenser and dabbed at the corners of her eyes.

"But you're at least thinking about it or else you wouldn't have objected to her getting a corgi for herself."

I was silent as I digested this. From one little comment I had made, Hannah had envisioned Jillian and me married and caring for a pack of corgis? I wasn't ready to get married again. I know Jillian wasn't. But ... maybe there was something there. Maybe Hannah was right. Was I already picturing the two of us starting a life together?

I shook my head. It was too soon. And waaayyy too fast.

"Okay, you've told me what she likes," I said, anxious to change the subject. "What doesn't she like?"

Hannah sat back in her chair and was silent for a few moments.

"Smokers. She doesn't like anything having to do with cigarettes, or cigars, or even those new electronic smokeless cigarettes. I think she's just anti-smoking."

"That's fine by me," I assured her. "I can't stand it in any way, shape, or form, either."

"Black licorice. She detests it. Don't make jokes or try to slip a piece into something else. It'll make her sick."

"No black licorice," I intoned as I jotted it down. "Got it."

"Horror movies. Anything that scares her, or makes her scream, she avoids."

"She doesn't like to be scared?" I asked, surprised. "So is she okay with blood and guts in a movie? I would have thought that would have been the clincher."

Hannah vehemently shook her head. "Eww, no. Of course not. Look, it's simple. Avoid anything that falls under the 'horror' genre and you'll be fine, regardless of what the movie actually contains."

"What about psychological thrillers?" I asked. "Those are bound to make you scream."

"I know there's a lot of gray area in there," Hannah admitted. "The only advice I can give you is that as long as it's not 'horror' then you're fine."

"Got it. A bit vague, but I'm good."

"Still at a loss?" Hannah prompted.

"Completely."

"Well, we'll have to think of something soon. It's less than two weeks before Christmas. You've waited until the last minute to ask for help. If you would have come to me sooner then I could probably have come up with ... wait a moment. How good are you on a computer?"

"I'm a writer. I'd say pretty darn good."

"Then I have an idea for you. You'll have to work fast, but if you can pull it off, I guarantee you'll make Jillian cry. In a good way."

I nodded. "You're on. What do I need to do?"

A few minutes later, I tucked my notebook into my pocket. I polished off my soda and tossed it into the trash bin. Hannah did the same for her drink. Together we headed outside. It was a balmy 58 degrees F today. I say 'balmy' because for us, it is. I'm told it's usually in the mid-40s by this time of year. Either way, I had a light jacket on while Hannah had bundled herself in a winter coat and had even wrapped a scarf around her neck.

I held the door open for her as we left the café.

"Where are you off to now, Zack?" Hannah asked.

"I'm headed back to the house. I need to edit the rough draft to my latest book. My editor is waiting for it and, as she keeps reminding me, if I don't get it to her within the next four days then I won't be able to get it published by Christmas."

Hannah looked at me and all but squealed with excitement.

"Tell me you're talking about the sequel to The Misty Rains! Tell me! Is it? Oh, tell me it is!"

I found it extremely unsettling, being able to talk to someone besides Samantha about my writing. I was so used to hiding under my alias that I wasn't sure how to handle talking about my work to someone that was, in essence, a stranger to me. Then again, I saw how excited she was and I smiled.

"The Misty Moors is set to be released a week before

Christmas," I confirmed.

Hannah clapped her hands excitedly.

"That's wonderful news! Tell me, how have you handled the disappearance of Megan, Amanda's little sister?"

I grinned again.

"If I told you that then that'd give it away, wouldn't it?"

"Oh, come on! Give me a hint! Just a teeny, tiny, miniscule clue. Give me something!"

I leaned forward and dropped my voice to a whisper.

"Can you keep a secret?"

"Of course!" Hannah nodded eagerly.

"Good. So can I."

Hannah swatted me on the arm.

"Spoilsport. Very well. I'll wait just like everyone else. This is so exciting. You've given me so much to look forward to this Christmas!"

I had to be careful to keep the surprise out of my eyes. It was just a book. News about an upcoming title shouldn't be that exciting. Clearly Ms. Bloom needed all the distractions she could get her hands on.

It was a sad way to live, if you ask me. I felt bad for her, but I couldn't let my face show it. Thinking quickly, I turned to her and smiled.

"You said that you've read all my books?"

Hannah nodded. "Every one. Many of them more than once."

"Do you have hardcovers on all of them?" I asked.

"No, only a few. I've read most of them on my tablet."

"Tell you what. As a way of saying thanks, I'll give you signed hard copies of whichever books you don't have, so it'll complete your collection. I'll even personalize them, if you'd like. Plus, I'll give your name and address to my publisher so you can be added to a very small group of people who receive ARCs."

"Omigod! That'd be so awesome! Thank you so much! Umm, what's an arc?"

"An ARC, in this context, is an acronym. It stands for advanced reader copy. It's a pre-release of the novel before it hits the stores. The understanding is once the book is officially published then the ARC team would go in and leave reviews. Some online retailers really do look at the number of reviews and it plays a significant part on how often my book is recommended when you're looking at other titles."

"Is that how that works?" Hannah asked, amazed. "I had always wondered about that."

"Some do, some don't. It's a real mystery. The only thing we know for sure is what has worked for us in the past. So, if you're interested, I'll add you to my ARC team. What do you say?"

Hannah lunged forward to catch me in a hug.

"Thank you so much! Of course I accept!"

An elderly couple, who just happened to be walking by, stopped next to us and smiled.

"Congratulations, you two," the older woman said. "You look so happy together!"

Right about then I'm sure Hannah and I looked like matching Coke cans. She blushed, I blushed, and before I could correct the friendly older couple, they had continued down the street. I shook my head.

"Well, that was awkward. Apparently we're engaged now."

"I'm sorry about that," Hannah apologized. "I shouldn't have hugged you."

I waved off her concerns, "Forget about it. I'm not concerned with what some old man and woman think about us. You're married and I'm seeing Jillian. All is good."

An hour later, I was busy pecking away on my computer when I heard a knock at the door. Sherlock and Watson, who had been asleep on the couch, were on their feet in seconds. Frantic barking sounded from across the hall as I hurried to the door. Sherlock was running laps around me while Watson followed discreetly from behind.

I opened the door to find a young kid holding a big heavy suitcase and a bottle of wine.

"Zack. Good. I'm glad you're here. I've got something to run by you."

I let the kid in. This kid, however, wasn't really a kid. He was Caden Burne, winemaster of my private winery, Lentari Cellars. My eyes narrowed as I saw the bottle. What did he have up his sleeve? He knew I hated wine and, thus far, hadn't been able to find one—be it red or white—that I could stomach. I managed to catch sight of the label. It was one of the types of white wine that Lentari Cellars made, Gewürztraminer. Swell. He was going to pester me until I tried it, and knowing me, I'll probably cave. Might as well get this over with.

Caden followed me back to my office. I have a small fridge next to my desk, for extreme emergencies. This one qualified. I pulled a soda out, cracked it open, and eyed the bottle.

"Ready."

"Oh, come on. It's not that bad. I swear, dude. I'll get you liking wine yet."

"Not likely. What have you got there?"

Caden carefully set his suitcase down on the ground

and opened it, revealing rows of small bottles. Curious, I spun in my chair and scooted closer. The two corgis also came in the room to see what I was doing. Sherlock sidled up to the open luggage and stuck his nose in amongst the bottles.

"What's in there?" I asked, concerned. "Anything a dog shouldn't be around?"

Caden shook his head. "No, it's fine. I've got some ideas for creating a new recipe for our next harvest."

"What's with all the bottles?" I asked, as I pointed at the neat rows of tiny vials sunk into thick black Styrofoam.

"They're ingredients," Caden explained. He pulled one of the vials out, unscrewed the lid, and offered it to me. "Smell this. Careful. It's strong."

I took the small glass vial and studied the contents. I could see dried twigs of some flowering plant. I cautiously sniffed. I was instantly reminded of pine trees, with a floral undertone.

"What is it?" I asked.

"You don't recognize it? It's lavender."

"And you want to put that in a wine?"

Caden shook his head. "Heavens, no. No flowers in our wine. That was just an example. I was thinking about making a special holiday mix."

"Just in time for Christmas," I said, nodding. "Smart."

"Christmas of next year," Caden clarified. "You don't rush making wine. In fact, here at Lentari Cellars we allow our wines to age…?"

My winemaster trailed off and looked expectantly at me. The little punk was testing me. I sat back and thought about it.

"One to three weeks."

"Nope. One to three months."

"Whoa."

"Once it ferments then it's really up to us to determine how long we'll allow it to age. I typically give them a month before we crack into a bottle to see how it's doing. If all goes well, we can release our holiday collection just before Thanksgiving. What do you say?"

I nodded. "It sounds good to me. What do you need from me?"

"Nothing, really. Well, that's not true. I need to borrow your taste buds."

"You're so barking up the wrong tree for a respectable opinion," I muttered. I took a large swallow from my soda and swished it around my mouth.

"Relax. I think you'll actually enjoy this. Remember those tempranillo vines I ordered last month?"

"Tempra-what vines?"

"Tempranillo. They're a variety of black grapes that originated in Spain. They can grow all over the country. I could have picked some up in California but I wanted us to have an edge. So I ordered a dozen vines straight from a buddy of mine who owns a vineyard in Barcelona."

"Impressive. Wait. Was this why you needed me to approve a $1500 agricultural purchase last month?"

Caden nodded. "Right. You can get the vines a lot cheaper locally, but I wanted the real thing. So these are imported vines."

"How are they growing?" I asked.

"Quite well. They should be ready for harvesting next year."

"Wait. Didn't you tell me that vines take longer than that to mature?"

"Nicely done, Zack. They do indeed. That's why we paid extra. Our vines were already well on their way to maturing. Now, I'd like to add a few things to the Tempranillo."

For the next hour and a half Caden pulled various bottles and presented them to me. He even had me sniff some of the ingredients in a very specific order while others were sampled at the same time. Once Caden was satisfied with our choices he packed up his vials and left.

Shaking my head—and still not really knowing what I'd just agreed to—I returned to my writing. Or, more specifically, I returned to my editing. I glanced at the clock and groaned. I really needed to finish polishing my rough draft and, at the rate I was going, I would never make my deadline. Time to buckle down.

As was typical whenever my nose was plastered in front of a computer screen, huge chunks of time would manage to slip by me. Three hours cruised by. However, at least I could say that it was finished. I saved a copy on my computer and emailed a copy to my editor. That ought to keep her off my back for a while longer.

My cell rang. A quick glance at the display had me frowning. It was my mother. I knew immediately what this call was about and how it was going to end.

"Hey, Mom. What's up?"

Dana Anderson was a retired psychologist who had spent many an hour dealing with clients at her own private practice. To say I had been thoroughly analyzed when I was a child would have been a serious understatement. I honestly didn't know how my father put up with it.

Speaking about my father, let me tell you about him real quick. Even though my mother made enough money for the both of them, William Anderson insisted on contributing to the family, so he had taken his love of sports cars and made a business out of it. Like my mother, he had clients, too, only these people were all over the world. Thanks to the help of modern technology, people would simply call him up, or contact him through his website, and tell him what their dream car was. My dad's job was to find it.

Now, it may sound simple, but once he tracked down the car then he had to oversee the sale, shipment, insurance, and a slew of other things I never knew about, before the car could be delivered to its new owner. At the same time I was moving out of Phoenix, he was overseeing the shipment of a 1967 Shelby Mustang to a buyer in Melbourne, Australia. Sweet car.

But, I digress. Back to the phone call.

I'm certain my mom was going to try—yet again—to get me to agree to come home for the holidays. It just wasn't going to happen. It was still too painful for me to be in Phoenix. The memories of Samantha were still too recent. I couldn't do it, and it galled me to know that my mother was still trying. I took a deep breath and returned my attention to the phone.

"Is everything okay with Dad?"

"Your dad is just fine, Zachary. He sends his love."

I laughed. "Dad would never say that."

"Not in those words, no, but you know what I mean."

"I do. What's on your mind, Mom?"

"What? Nothing, of course. Can't a mother call up her son to see how he's doing?"

"Not when you're trying, yet again, to get me to come home for Christmas," I pointed out. "I told you before and I'll tell you again, I'm just not ready for that. So I will have to pass, thank you very much."

"Zachary, you belong home," my mother quietly told me. "Your father and I both agree. You shouldn't be living by yourself so far away. It isn't right."

"Mom, we've been through this. I inherited a winery from Samantha's family. I'm keeping it open in her honor. End of story."

"But you're all alone out there!" my mother protested.

"Who says I'm alone?" I automatically responded. A split second later I groaned as I realized my mistake. I had yet to tell my parents that I was seeing anyone. Knowing my mother as well as I did, she was going to go completely bonkers on me.

"What? You're not?! Who are you seeing? Why haven't you told me? Why would you hide this from me?"

"Mom, please. Don't read too much into this."

"Why haven't you told me about any of this?"

"Because I'm over eighteen and I don't have to."

"Who is she?" my mother demanded. "What's her name?"

"For the sake of everyone's wellbeing, she will remain anonymous," I cryptically answered.

"Why? Why won't you tell me?"

"Because the last thing I need you to do is to get involved. Look, Mom. I'll be honest. I didn't think I'd ever be able to think about dating again once I lost Samantha. Now, all of a sudden, I find that I'm open to the idea. So I'm taking baby steps. I ... totally sounded just like you. That's just great. Well, I hope you're happy."

My mother laughed.

"Oh, I'm so proud of you, Zachary. Why don't you bring her down here so we can meet her?"

"Oh, no," I vowed.

"You will," my mom promised. "You'll see."

"Have a good day, Mom."

* * *

Later that night, being a Friday, found Jillian and me on our usual 'date night' outing. I had wanted to go to Casa de Joe's, hands down the best Mexican restaurant I have ever stepped foot into in my life. Coming from someone who used to live in Phoenix, that's saying something. I should also mention that the owner, Joe Cantolli, is Italian, so I'm not sure how he does it. Maybe his wife is Mexican? I don't care. As long as his restaurant continues to pump out dishes that would make a Mexican native green with envy, I didn't question or complain.

Unfortunately, Jillian wanted to get me out of my comfort zone. She suggested we try someplace new. She, of course, has had dinner at every restaurant here in town. I, on the other hand, had quickly created a short list of favorite places to go and rarely ventured anywhere else. Jillian was determined to destroy that list.

At approximately 5:30 p.m., I parked my Jeep in front of Marauder's Grill. Jillian's SUV was already here. I also feel I should point out that there was only one other car in the parking lot. The cook's? This didn't bode well.

I looked at the restaurant and shook my head. It looked as though someone had built a tiny shack sometime in the last century, had abandoned it, and now some whack-a-doodle entrepreneur had decided to set up shop inside. Clearly their decorating budget had been non-existent.

I grudgingly pulled open the front door and stepped inside. I inhaled and promptly forgot about all my concerns.

I could smell a charcoal grill. Appetizing scents of roast meat, barbecued chicken, smoked sausages, and probably a slew of other items I couldn't place smacked me senseless.

"Zachary!" Jillian called out from the tiny dining room. "Over here!"

I moved over to the tiny table and sat down on a rickety chair.

"I was about ready to suggest you were off your rocker for coming here, but if the food is half as good as it smells, I may have found my new favorite restaurant. I can't believe it's as slow as it is. What's wrong with people? Don't their noses work?"

"Look at the size of this dining room," Jillian said as she looked around. "You'd barely fit four full-sized families in here. Most people have learned to place carry out orders. Do you see the grill over there?"

Jillian pointed at a huge circular hearth. I'm sure I was drooling as I studied the open grill. Ribs, and chicken, and sausages ... oh, my! I think I've died and gone to carnivore heaven. Jillian pulled a napkin off the dispenser, leaned forward, and dabbed my mouth with it.

"Was I drooling?" I asked, grinning. I made a show of wiping the back of my arm across my mouth.

"Just a little."

"So what's good here?" I asked.

"Pretty much everything as long as you're not a vegan," Jillian assured me. "And if you are, they've been known to lure a vegan or two back to the dark side."

"I love your references to sci-fi and fantasy," I told her.

Jillian smiled and raised her glass of tea in mock salute. A waitress wandered by and we placed our orders. I threw caution out the window and ordered a whole rack of ribs.

Turns out the ribs came with a grilled ear of corn. It also had
French fries, but I ignored them. The ribs were screaming
my name. Jillian ordered the prime rib—medium—with a
side of grilled mushrooms.

It was fantastic. As we ate, I gave her a recap of how
my day went, finishing with the frustrating call from my
mother. I looked at her, after I finished, and sighed.

"How do you do it?"

"How do I do what?" Jillian asked.

"How do you put up with the holidays?"

"What do you mean?"

"For me, it's depressing. I lost Sam just before
Thanksgiving."

"That explains why you were moping around here last
week," Jillian said, nodding. "I suspected it might have had
something to do with Samantha's death, but I didn't want
to say anything."

"I'll be honest," I continued. "I was dreading the
holidays coming up. You were right. I wasn't myself around
Thanksgiving, even though you were doing everything you
could to cheer me up. Now that Christmas is approaching,
I felt myself starting to slide back into depressedville, even
though I don't want to."

"Are you asking how I manage to stay in a good mood
for Christmas, Zachary?"

"Well, yeah. I guess so."

"The short answer is, I don't."

"Huh? But you're always so chipper!"

"That's the face I put on for the outside world to see,"
Jillian explained. "It's still hard for me. There are days I
don't want to get out of bed. But ... I still do. I don't want
to be known as 'that lonely old widow.' I live my life as I'm

sure Michael would have wanted me to. It's all I can do, Zachary."

"You're going to have to teach me how to do that."

"The next WW class is this coming Wednesday. You need to come with me."

"The next WW class?" I repeated, confused. "You're a member of Weight Watchers, too?"

Jillian's eyebrows shot up, as did every red flag I own. Time to practice my backpedaling skills.

"Umm, perhaps I should have asked what the WW stands for?"

"Widows and Widowers, you silly man. It's for people who have lost their spouses. Most attendees are much older than us, but there are some who are in our age bracket."

"Sounds like a real hoot."

"You wanted to know how I dealt with my pain. That's how I do it."

"Fair enough. We'll see. So what do you usually do for Christmas? If your parents aren't here, then do you fly out to wherever they are?"

Jillian shook her head. "I usually just work. I find the holidays supremely boring. I'd much rather spend my time at my store. Last year I offered a Christmas cookie decorating class."

"Are you thinking about doing the same this year?"

Jillian gave me a sidelong glance and smiled demurely.

"No. I have no plans of working this year."

Right on cue, my face flushed bright red. Just as the waiter dropped off the check, which I snatched away before Jillian could grab it, my phone rang. I scowled. If this was my mother again, then she and I were going to have a serious disagreement. I looked at my phone and relaxed. It was Vance.

"Do you mind?" I asked. I held my phone up so she could see the display.

"Not at all."

"Hey, Vance. What's up?"

"Zack. What are you doing right now?"

"It's Friday. I'm..."

"Oh, that's right. Casa de Joe's. My bad. Listen, do you have any plans for the rest of the night?"

Jerk. I wasn't that predictable, was I? I eyed Jillian and tried to get the frown off my face.

"Possibly. What's going on? Are you okay?"

"Do you think I could get you and the dogs to do me a favor?"

"Uh-oh. What's wrong? What happened?"

"There's been a burglary. A damned odd one. I could use another set of eyes. And maybe a nose or two."

TWO

"I wish I could say that this was the first crime scene I have ever seen," I remarked as soon as I ducked under a familiar strip of yellow tape and stepped foot into the small apartment. Sherlock and Watson followed me in. "But we both know that'd be a lie."

Vance, who had his back to me and had been chatting with one of the crime scene techs—an overweight man in his thirties—turned at the sound of my voice and waved me over. We were standing in the small living room of a tiny two-bedroom apartment on the northern side of town. I remember driving by this apartment complex a few times, back when I didn't know the town and had become lost. It was a smaller complex, with maybe twenty apartments divvied up into three buildings, and a fourth, smaller building acting as office and recreational center. It also had a pool, but judging by the color of the water, I wouldn't dip a toe in it. Water should never be green.

I looked around the little living room.

"Who lives here?"

Vance turned to point out through the open front door.

"They do. Look outside and you'll see the Murphy family, party of four."

I turned to see a young family huddled closely together outside. They were being interviewed by a uniformed police officer. The two children were staring at us inside. Or, more specifically, they were staring at Sherlock and Watson. Sherlock was ignoring the kids and was glancing around the sparse furnishings while Watson had decided to sit down by my right foot and watch the proceedings with minimal effort. I caught her throwing looks out the door to see what the kids were doing.

Deciding I should walk around the living room and actually do that which Vance had asked me to, I gave Sherlock some extra slack on his leash and encouraged him to explore. As we investigated the apartment, I couldn't help but notice how this family was going to be hurting after this incident. There wasn't a lot of money in this apartment. A worn sofa, discolored recliner, and a heavily scratched coffee table met my eyes. I returned my attention to the living room and the decorated tree in the corner. For whatever inexplicable reasons, Vance had explained to me, the thief had only taken the presents from under the tree. And, from the looks of things, they had been thorough. There wasn't a single gift anywhere in sight.

I glanced back around the room to see if I could tell if anything else had been taken. There, on the rickety assemble-it-yourself entertainment center, were the few electronics that the family owned. They were still there. An old 25-inch CRT TV was the focal point, with a dusty, grimy VCR sitting forlornly on a shelf to the left of the television. A few torn VHS dust jackets were all that I could see in the storage cabinet directly below the TV. In case you were wondering how I managed to acquire x-ray vision, I can confirm I didn't. The cabinet below the television was missing a door.

Vance appeared by my side.

"They didn't steal any of the electronics," he softly informed me.

"Look at that thing," I responded, hooking a thumb in the TV's direction. "It's a dinosaur. They don't even sell those box televisions any more. I wouldn't give you ten bucks for it."

"There's a VCR deck that's seen better days," Vance mused. "Still, as far as the homeowner can tell, nothing was stolen except for the presents under the tree."

"Those must have been some presents," I decided.

"Hardly," Vance scoffed. "Look at this place, Zack. This is a family that's living paycheck-to-paycheck. They didn't have extra money, and if they did, they spent it on their kids."

"How do you know that?" I asked.

Vance frowned and crossed his arms over his chest, "Because I'm a father. I can tell. Look around this place. What little they have is all geared toward their children. Besides, all of the presents were for the kids."

"Do we know what kind of presents they were?" I asked.

Vance nodded and pulled out his notebook.

"A few dolls for the girl. There was a handheld video game for the boy. A few toy trucks and some sort of Lego set. That's it."

"Nothing really worth stealing," I mused.

"It gets better. Richard—the father—said there was no sign of forced entry. It doesn't appear the locks have been messed with. I've already talked with the tenants above and below this unit. No one has reported any suspicious activity. No noises. Not even anyone loitering around the area. I'm at a loss here."

"Did you check to see if anyone has a key to this place besides them? Like a friend, or a relative?"

Vance nodded. "I've already asked, and the answer is no. Both the mother and father have keys. I made them show them to me, just to be certain they were still there. There is the manager's master key, and that's presently locked up in the manager's office. Only the manager and the assistant manager have access. Before you ask, both have alibis, which have also checked out. It was neither of them. The extra keys are secured in a lockbox in the back office. All of those keys were accounted for, too. No signs of tampering, either."

"So, their presents up and vanished right from under everyone's noses?" I asked, confused. "How is that even possible?"

"Now you know why you and the dogs are here. Get Sherlock to work his magic. I'd like to see what he can find."

"We've been around the living room a few times," I told my friend. "The only thing Sherlock has shown the slightest interest in is the tree."

"What about the tree?" Vance wanted to know.

We both walked over to the corner of the living room where a surprisingly vibrant and healthy dark blue-green Christmas tree met our eyes. It was about five feet tall, uniformly pyramid-shaped, and had a pleasant scent. And I have to admit that it looked mighty barren without any presents under it.

As Vance and I stared at the tree, I glanced out the window at the young family. The parents were embracing their kids in a four-way hug and slowly rocking back and forth. I felt bad. Kids should have something to wake up to on Christmas morning. That was half the fun of being a kid.

"What's he doing?" Vance suddenly asked.

I glanced down at Sherlock. The tri-color corgi had ducked under the tree's canopy and was circling behind the tree. Either I had to let go of the leash or else Sherlock was going to find himself attached to the trunk.

"It's just a tree, pal," I told the corgi. "What's the matter? Not used to seeing a tree indoors?"

Sherlock froze in mid-step. He gave me an unreadable expression before he looked up at the tree. I watched him cock his head, as if he had heard something he couldn't identify.

"There's nothing there but needles, pal," I told the corgi. "Come on, we really should … before I do that, are we allowed?"

"Are you allowed to what?" Vance asked.

"Are we allowed to look around the apartment? I mean, from the look of things, the crook only visited the living room. Do we have permission to look around?"

"You can look wherever you want," a new voice said.

I glanced over at the door and saw the young father

standing in the doorway, looking down at Sherlock. One of the uniformed policemen moved to block his way. Sherlock looked over at the man and then up at me, as if to say that he had heard the tenant give permission.

"Mr. Murphy," I heard Vance say as I led the dogs from the living room, "do you have any idea how someone could get in here? You said that you and your wife were working today. The kids were in school. That would suggest someone came in here in the middle of the day and took the gifts?"

I could still hear the conversation as Sherlock, Watson, and I moved around the apartment. The father was in a state of denial. I heard the father confirm what Vance had told me. They were struggling to live paycheck-to-paycheck. I didn't hear him say anything about how worried he was about his kids but I could hear it in the father's voice. The last thing I heard before Vance and the man dropped their voices was an offer, from Vance, to put the family in touch with an organization or two that might be able to help.

I returned my attention to the investigation. The dogs and I slowly explored the entire apartment. The only time Sherlock showed any signs of interest was whenever we were in the living room. More specifically, the little tri-color corgi only had eyes for that tree. He always returned to the trunk to sniff around the base and then to gaze admiringly up at the foliage above his head.

"Anything?" Vance called.

"No," I glumly reported. "He keeps returning to the tree. I personally think he's fascinated by a tree being indoors. I mean, he's a dog after all."

"Oooo, what pretty dogs!" I heard a young female voice say.

I turned to see the daughter, maybe five or six, squat down and hold out a hand. Thinking they were being offered treats, Sherlock and Watson immediately hurried over. Within moments Watson was rolling around on the floor, presenting her furry belly for a free scratch. Sherlock sat next to the girl and watched her like a hawk. The girl looked up at me and smiled, displaying two missing front teeth.

"They're so cute! I love your dogs, mister."

"And they love the attention," I returned.

"What are their names?" the boy asked. He looked to be seven or eight.

"The one laying spread-eagled right there, without a shred of modesty, is Watson. That's Sherlock over there, sitting quietly and watching his roommate beg for a belly rub."

"Sherlock and Watson," the father repeated, giving us a meek smile. "Cute names. Are you finished here? Can the kids come back inside?"

Vance looked over at me. He looked down at the dogs and nodded at the door. It was time to leave.

"Thanks for trying," Vance told me as we headed back toward the parking lot.

As soon as both of us were back on the ground floor, having just come down the flight of steps leading up to the second story, we set the dogs down. Vance had generously carried Watson down while I carried Sherlock. I realize that corgis have short legs, and I think both dogs were willing to try navigating the stone steps on their own, but I figured it was just easier to carry them. That way no one risked injury.

"Where are you off to now?" I asked my friend.

"Back to the station. I'm going to go through the case files and see if this burglary matches up with any other cases, recent or otherwise. There's something strange going on here. There had to be a reason why that apartment was targeted. What about you?"

"I have a few phone calls to make."

"Well, have fun."

We parted ways. I put both dogs in my Jeep and we took off. Just as soon as we pulled out of the complex, I hit my hands-free telephone button on my stereo.

"Greetings, Zachary," my phone politely said. "What can I do for you today?"

"I need the number to The Toy Closet."

"There are no contacts in your address book that match that name," my phone told me after a brief silence.

"I know that. Would you please look it up?"

"Would you like me to search for that contact on the internet?" my phone asked.

"Yes, please."

"One moment. All right, Zachary, I found three entries that matched your description. Would you like to hear them?"

I rolled my eyes. This ought to be good.

"Yes."

"I found White Glove Home Cleaning, located in Medford, Oregon. Would you like to call the number, get directions, or neither?"

"Neither. I'm not looking for a cleaner. Try again."

"The second search result is Sin-Sational, located in Medford, Oregon. Would you like to call the number, get directions, or neither?"

"That sounds like an adult store, you lily-livered hunk

of junk. No, I don't want to call them."

"Would you like to call the number, get directions, or neither?" my phone repeated.

"Neither!"

"The third search result is The Toy Closet, located in Pomme Valley, Oregon. Would you like to…"

I cut the phone off as I hastily pressed the 'call' button I saw on the phone's display.

"Thank you for calling Toy Closet, this is Woody. How can I help you?"

"Woody, this is Zack Anderson. Do you remember me?"

"Zack! Of course I do! You're everyone's favorite winery owner. What can I do for you, buddy?"

"You sell all kinds of toys there, don't you?"

"I most certainly do. I've got something for everyone, covering all age brackets. Why do you ask?"

"Well, I'm hoping you can do me a favor."

"Hit me with your best. Whatcha need?"

"I was just at a crime scene," I began. "I…"

"Boy, there's a shocker," Woody interrupted. "You sure do seem to enjoy your crime scenes. Which one were you at this time?"

"It's not like I search these things out," I complained. "They always seem to find me. Anyway, I was just at the scene of a home burglary. Someone broke into this young family's home and stole all their Christmas presents."

I could tell that I now had Woody's attention.

"Oh, that sucks. How can I help?"

"Well, there are two kids who call that little apartment home. A boy and a girl. I'd like you to pick out some toys for them so they'll have something to open on Christmas day. Don't worry about the bill. I'll cover it."

"That's generous of you. How much are you looking to spend?"

"Umm, I don't know. I haven't really shopped for kids before. Do you think $100 apiece would be enough to get them some cool stuff?"

"A hundred? Per kid? You're telling me you're prepared to spend $200 on two kids you don't know?"

"It's my favorite time of year," I explained. "I hate to see someone hurting, especially when they are struggling. So, is that enough?"

"For $200, not only will I guarantee each child will have a fantastic Christmas, but I'll even throw in a few things that mom and dad ought to love."

"Just promise me if you go over the $200, then you'll let me know so I can pay you for it, okay?"

"Sure thing. I'll even do one better. I'll throw in a gift-wrapping service. All the presents will be properly wrapped by an expert."

"You wrap presents, too?"

"Who, me? Not a chance. If you'd like to see what a gift wrapped in newspaper and duct tape looks like, then I'm your man. Otherwise I'll pass you to the pro."

"Who?" I asked, curious.

"Zoe."

"Your daughter, right? Will she be okay with wrapping a bunch of presents for me?"

"Oh, she will be," Woody promised. "Service with a smile."

Zoe was a very precocious twelve-year-old and was known to help her father out in the store on the weekends. I've had a few interactions with her, but on those times that I have spoken with her, she'd always smile and was never too shy to offer an opinion whenever I asked her a question. She also happened to love Sherlock and Watson and has puppy sat for them on more than one occasion.

"That'd be perfect, Woody. Tell Zoe I appreciate all her help."

"Oh, she won't be volunteering her time. I guarantee you that she'll charge me for it."

"Oh. Well, if you'll tell me how much she..."

"Zack, don't worry about it. You're buying presents for the family. Let me at least arrange to get them properly gift-wrapped. It's the least I can do."

"Thanks, Woody. I will then. I appreciate it. I'll swing by tomorrow afternoon to settle up."

"Sounds like a plan."

My next call was to the owner of the best bakery in town. Well, if you want to get technical, they were the only bakery in town: Farmhouse Bakery. It just so happened that the owner, Taylor Adams, was a good friend of Jillian's. I might not have known her that well, but as was the case in a small town like PV, she knew my dogs better than she knew me. Hopefully she'd be able to grant me a favor, too.

"Farmhouse Bakery. Can I help you?"

"I'm looking for Taylor Adams."

"Speaking. What can I do for you?"

"Taylor, this is Zack Anderson. I'm a friend of..."

"Zachary Anderson! You don't need to introduce yourself! I know who you are. What can I do for you? Do you need more doggie treats? Stop by any time. They're on the house."

"Actually, I have a favor to ask of you, Taylor."

"Is this for Jillian's birthday next month? Just tell me

what you need. I'd be delighted to help."

Jillian's birthday was next month? I had completely forgotten. I hastily made a mental note to add it to my calendar, knowing full well that by the time I got home it'd be long forgotten.

"Actually no, this isn't about Jillian."

"Oh? What can I do for you?"

"I don't know if you've heard, but a young family was burglarized earlier today. They have two small kids living in that apartment. I was hoping to get some cookies or cupcakes delivered to them. Anonymously, of course."

"That's awful sweet of you. I have just the thing. I just decorated a fresh batch of peppermint flavored vanilla and chocolate cupcakes. I'll put together a selection and have Megan run them over."

Megan was a high school junior who worked part time at the bakery.

"Hmm, I have several dozen sugar cookies that have yet to be decorated. Are the children boys or girls?"

"There's one of each. The girl looks like she's around five and the boy is not that much older."

"Got it. I'll take care of this."

"Just let me know how much it'll be and I'll be in to take care of it."

"Absolutely not. This is on me. I don't like to see families hurting this time of year. If I can help put a smile on their face then that's all the payment I need."

"I didn't call you up to ask for a handout," I reminded her. "I'm just trying to help out this family. It's a secret Santa type of thing."

"And I am helping you out by contributing. End of story, Zack."

"Look, maybe we could…"

"Do I have to call Jillian and tell her that you're being unreasonable?" Taylor asked, with a hint of laughter in her voice.

"Tell you what. I'll buy a dozen cupcakes and maybe a dozen cookies. If there's anything you'd like to secretly add to that order, then I won't object."

"It's a deal, Zack. When would you like these to be delivered?"

"Umm, I'd say as soon as you can get them over there. I'll swing by tomorrow afternoon and square up with you then. Would that be okay?"

"That'd be perfect, Zack. Thanks for letting me help."

"Thanks for volunteering. This whole small-town atmosphere takes some getting used to."

"You're from Phoenix, right?"

"That's right."

"They don't look out for one another in the big city?"

"Not like this, they don't. At least they never did in my neighborhood."

"Well, you'd better get used to it, Zachary. We take care of each other in PV."

"Thanks, Taylor. I'll be by within the next day or so to settle up."

"I'll see you then, Zack."

I hung up the phone and eyed the dogs. I had rolled each of the back windows down just enough where they could stick their heads out to enjoy the fresh air, but not enough where they could possibly fall out. Watson hadn't figured it out yet but Sherlock knew where the window controls were and also knew how to use it. As a result, I had to keep the windows locked at all times. At the moment, both dogs had their heads poked outside the windows and were spraying flecks of drool all down my Jeep.

Oh, the joys of being a dog owner.

Sherlock had just pulled his head back inside when he let out a warning woof. Naturally, that caused Watson to start woofing, too. Several seconds later the soft woofs had escalated into full-fledged barks. My gaze returned to the road. We were driving east along Main Street and had just passed Watt's Veterinary Clinic & Animal Shelter, owned and operated by my friend, Harrison Watt. The building was dark, but then again, it wasn't surprising seeing how it was past 6:00 p.m. on a Friday night. So the question was, what was Sherlock barking at this time? He hadn't barked at Harry's office in quite some time. A quick scan up and down the street revealed there wasn't anyone walking alongside the road.

"What are you guys barking at, you goofballs? There's no one there. If you're barking at Harry's place, then you're a couple of hours too late. He's closed."

Sherlock ignored me. It was then that I noticed that he and Watson were both sticking their heads out the same window, on the right side of the Jeep. I took my foot off the accelerator and allowed the car to slow. I smiled. I'm pretty sure I just figured out what had set Sherlock off.

We were now passing Gary's Grocery and its huge parking lot. We were also passing the site of a demolition zone. The old Square L convenience store was being prepared to be torn down. Gary, owner of the town's only grocery store, had bought the small store with the intention of ripping it down and adding the extra space to his parking lot. As a result a large bulldozer, a backhoe, and two dump trucks were parked within the perimeter of a temporary chain link fence. There was also a windowless white cargo van parked off to the side. Perhaps Gary had rented a van to take one last load of stuff out of the doomed store? Either that or else there was a kidnapper hiding out in PV. Wasn't that the type of van that those creeps always seemed to use?

I should also clarify that I was pretty certain Sherlock wasn't barking at the heavy machinery. The equipment had been parked for the weekend and that corner of the huge parking lot was all dark and quiet. No, the reason Sherlock had been barking at the Square L was because nearly two months ago everyone had thought a mummy had come back to life and had stolen a priceless pendant.

All right. Stop your scoffing. It was just me, okay? I was the one that had been convinced we had an undead perpetrator walking around town. As it turns out, the mummy side of things had been an elaborate ruse to steal a valuable, ugly, Egyptian pendant. It may sound strange, but the Square L store figured into the hoax.

I stared at the two corgis in the rear view mirror. The problem was, it didn't sound like Sherlock was bragging. It was more of a you-really-need-to-check-this-out-dad type of bark.

"There's no one in the store, Sherlock," I told the little corgi. "You already caught the bad guy and found the loot. You should be proud!"

The look of disgust Sherlock had on his face had me laughing out loud. From the way he was staring at me Sherlock must have thought I was the stupidest biped he ever had the misfortune of dealing with. Turns out he was right. More on that later.

THREE

I'm never going to remember any of this."

"It's not like I haven't been explaining what each of these machines do for the past two months, Zack."

I scowled at Caden. We were standing amidst all the sparkling complicated-looking machines that were responsible for producing all the wines that Lentari Cellars was known for. In fact, I was literally standing in the exact same position where I had discovered a dead body the first time I had investigated my newly inherited winery. Caden turned to point at the large vat that was closest to me.

"Quiz time, pal. What is this?"

"A, uh, fermenter?"

Caden nodded. "That's good. Which one?"

I paled. There was more than one? I glanced around

at the other machines all connected by pipes and tubing. Including the vat directly in front of me, there were five others nearby. All were identical in appearance. Well, at least they were to me. I did remember Caden saying something about his 2-2-2 rule. Something about three sets of two vats that each did something different. It all depended upon their place in the line. So, let's see. The fermenter was sitting the closest to a large, bulky machine that was nicknamed 'the crusher'. So that had to make it the stage 1 fermenter.

"Stage 1, right?"

Caden grinned broadly.

"Nicely done. Was that a guess or did you actually know?"

I walked over to the machine closest to the back loading bays and pointed at it.

"Well, this is the crusher, as I've heard you call it before. This is where the recently harvested grapes are dumped and then pressed." I paused to look over at Caden. My winemaster nodded, indicating I should continue. "Now, the vat that you just asked about is the first tank that the mulch is deposited into."

Caden's eyebrows shot up. "Mulch?"

"Yeah, mulch. Anyway, it then…"

Caden held up his hands in a time-out gesture.

"Hold up, we need to correct your vocabulary. It isn't called 'mulch'. Mulch is what you spread on the ground, around plants and such, in order to prevent erosion. 'Must' is freshly pressed wine juice which typically contains skins, seeds, and stems."

"Must," I repeated. "Not mulch. Got it. Thanks. Anyway, the must then travels from the crusher to this tank, the fermenter."

"And how long does it stay there?" Caden asked as he walked alongside of me.

"Hmm. A month?"

"Close. Anywhere from seven to fourteen days."

"I thought it fermented longer than that."

"Don't forget there's a second fermenter," Caden reminded me.

"Ah. So it sits in that fermenter for at least a month, right?"

"Nope. The must sits inside the second fermenter from three to seven days. I'm not sure why you keep saying months instead of days."

"That makes two of us."

"Then what happens to the must?" Caden asked. "What's next?"

I traced the stainless steel pipes coming out of the second fermenter over to a vat of equal size. However, this tank looked to be mobile. I smiled. I finally knew the answer to one of my test questions. I rapped my knuckles on the huge wooden barrel.

"This is one of the holding tanks. This is the part where it ages, right?"

Caden nodded. "That's right. We'll age the wine in these oak barrels, which each hold…?"

"Fifty gallons?"

"Sixty. And each barrel will typically produce how many bottles?"

"Okay, I know for a fact that we haven't covered this before," I pointed out.

Caden smiled. "True. I'm looking for a guess here. What do you think?"

"Sixty gallons," I mumbled to myself. "I heard somewhere that it takes about five bottles of wine to make a gallon. If that's true then each of these barrels would make around three hundred bottles. That's a lot of wine. That can't be right, can it?"

Caden slapped me on the back and let out a whoop.

"Nicely done, Zack! That's exactly right. Each sixty-gallon barrel will produce roughly three hundred 750ml bottles."

"And how many of these barrels do we produce each year?"

Caden led me away from the machinery, back toward the winery's storefront.

"There are a lot of variables that affect the yield of a vineyard. Space between vines, between the rows, the variety and age of the grapes, it all can affect how many grapes we get from each acre. A vineyard will typically produce anywhere from two to ten tons of grapes per acre. And, in case you're wondering, a single ton of grapes will yield approximately two barrels of wine."

"Holy moley!!" I whistled, amazed. "That's a lot of wine!"

"I've seen both lower and higher yields," Caden told me. "But in our case, we have been averaging just under two tons per acre."

"So how many acres do we have here?" I asked, genuinely curious.

"This is your land and you don't even know?" Caden asked as he smirked at me.

"I've got a lot on my plate right now," I grumbled. "Cut me a little slack, okay?"

"Yeah, tough life, buddy. Anyway, Lentari Cellars has

about fifteen acres dedicated to our vines."

"You're telling me that we produce thirty tons of grapes each year?"

Caden shook his head. "Not even close. Thirty tons would be sweet. Believe it or not, our target goal is much higher. I'd like to see all fifteen acres yielding at least five tons per acre."

"Oh, I get it. We may have fifteen acres but we're not using all the acres, is that right?"

"Yes."

"How many are we presently using?"

Caden shrugged. "Maybe a third? What's sad is that a mere two years ago I had all fifteen acres producing close to eight tons each. You can thank Ms. Bitch for scaling that down."

The bitch in question was Abigail Dawson, daughter of Bonnie Davies, the lady who bequeathed essentially everything she owned to me. Abigail resented the fact that I alone had taken control of the winery and hadn't been intimidated by her strong arm tactics to surrender control to her. She had tried to get me to sign over the house and the winery on more than one occasion and each time had been just as successful as the first.

I was also convinced Abigail, or at least one of her cronies, had been responsible for calling the house in the middle of the night. I can only assume she was trying to make my life miserable and I'd throw in the proverbial towel. All that ended up happening was that I got rid of the landline and resorted to using my cell phone for everything. So, against better judgment, I was becoming more and more adept at using my new-fangled smart phone.

"And how many acres were still usable when you took

over your duties as winemaster?" I asked.

"Less than three. It makes me sick to think that Lentari Cellars almost went under, all because the bitch was trying to wrest control away from her mother."

"You don't need to worry about that now," I told Caden. "She's out of the picture and you're not. That's all that matters."

"Do you have any questions for me?" Caden asked.

I smiled. As a matter of fact, I did. I pointed back toward the machines.

"At what point do you add the flavor to the wines?" I asked. "We produce three different types. How are each of them made? I can only assume it has something to do with that huge suitcase full of ingredients. At what point back there do you add these things? I guess I'd like to know how it's done."

Caden led me back amongst the machinery.

"Come on, I'll show you. Do you see this here?"

"That's the fermenter again."

"This is where the magic happens. I'm not talking about adding a little bit of this and a little of that to change a simple red wine over to a Syrah. Each type of wine has its own distinct recipe, its own distinct way to be made. Specific grapes, different amounts of yeast, and so on. No, what I'm talking about is personalizing the must, making it something that no one else has."

"Okay, hit me with your best. What do you do? What can you do?"

"Let's start with the obvious," Caden began. "Alcohol. Since we use fresh grapes then it's not unheard of to get fruit that has low sugar content. So, what do you do?"

"Call you," I suggested.

Caden grinned. "True. And what I'd do would be to employ a process called 'chaptalization'. It means you can increase the alcohol content by increasing the sugar. It's usually accomplished by adding more sugar, or honey, or even grape concentrate."

"I didn't know that was possible," I confessed.

"It's illegal in California and Italy," Caden told me.

"Seriously? What about here?"

"Perfectly legal," Caden assured me.

"And have you ever had to do that chapterization thing?"

"Chaptalization," Caden corrected. "And I have, but only to bring the alcohol content up to where it's supposed to be. I've never deliberately increased the alcohol levels to something other than what they should be."

"And out of sheer curiosity, what should they be?"

"A very precise 14.4 percent."

"And if it's above or below that?" I asked. "You're telling me there are ways to increase or decrease?"

Caden nodded. "Of course. I wouldn't be much of a winemaster if I couldn't control every facet of our wine's production, would I?"

"I guess not," I decided.

The more I thought about it the more I was glad I had managed to convince Caden to resume his duties here at the winery. There was no way on earth I'd be able to run this place. It's way too technical and precise for my tastes.

"You asked about flavoring. Well, aside from modifying the alcohol content, there's also the acidity factor, which controls tartness."

I nodded. I think that was the biggest issue I had with wine in general. It was way too tart for me.

"Then there's tannin," Caden continued. "You find

it more in red wine than white. It's what gives you that sandpaper feeling in your mouth."

Check that. That was what I hated about the wine.

"Then there's the body of the wine, which can be increased or decreased and there's the sweetness. I'm under the impression that no one really cares for a dry wine. That's probably what you don't like about wine, Zack."

"From the sounds of things, I think I must hate everything people love about wine. The taste, the smell, the alcohol... it's all just so, so, blech."

"Like I said, I'll get you to enjoy a bottle of wine yet."

"When pigs fly, pal."

"Not even if we make a dessert wine?"

Now he was fighting dirty. It was a well-known fact that I had a sweet tooth. I just didn't see how 'dessert' could possibly be used as an adjective for wine. I'm also sure my face must have reflected my skepticism.

"Don't look so cynical," Caden scolded. "Dessert wines are in high demand right now. I've been working on a recipe for quite some time now. I'm close to producing a viable sample. I've been itching to try it, only I'm trying to be patient. I haven't quite got the taste right yet. But I will. Soon."

"So try it out then," I instructed, "just leave my taste buds out of it."

Caden turned to me, his face becoming grim.

"Okay, here's the bet. You'll try the sample I'm working on. If you like it, and I'm trusting you to be honest, then you'll work with me to open up your taste buds and help me expand our line."

"And if I legitimately hate it?" I prompted. "What do I win?"

"I'll never ask you to taste test a wine again."

I thrust out a hand.

"Deal."

We were halfway into a conversation explaining how the bottler worked when my cell phone rang, only the ring was off. Something was different about it. Curious, I pulled my cell from my pocket and groaned. It was my mother.

Caden peered over my shoulder at my phone.

"Looks like she wants a face-to-face. No worries. I'll give you your privacy."

My mother wanted a what? Then I noticed that this wasn't a typical call. There was a message on the screen that said my mother was trying to initiate a video call.

Shoot me now.

I took a deep breath and hit the green 'receive' button.

"Mom. Hi. This is new. What's with the video call?"

"Can't a mother want to see her son's face?" my mother returned. "That's not asking too much, is it?"

I stared down at the face filling my phone's screen.

"As you probably know, this is my first video call. There's gotta be a reason for this, Mom. What is it?"

Maybe I was the worst son on the face of the planet, but there was something about this call that was annoying me. I had just talked to my mother yesterday, when she tried to guilt me into returning to Phoenix for Christmas. If I didn't know any better I'd say she was making a full-on attempt to get me to relocate back to Arizona.

"I just watched a movie and it got me thinking."

I headed back to the house while holding my phone out in front of me. I knew my mom was hoping I'd ask about the movie. Might as well get it over with.

"And what movie would that be?"

"My Last Christmas. Have you heard of it?"

I shook my head no.

"It's a good movie, Zachary."

I grunted, but elected to keep silent. I hadn't been asked a question yet so I wasn't about to volunteer any additional information. I knew I was being difficult, and a small part of my brain felt sorry about it, but I just knew that somehow this conversation was going to be twisted around until I started to feel like an ungrateful lout because I had no plans on coming 'home' for Christmas. Sorry, Mom. Home isn't in Phoenix anymore. It's right here, in Pomme Valley.

"Do you know who was in it?" my mother asked.

I studied her face. She had worry lines etched all across her features. Something was bugging her and I knew it didn't have anything to do with the movie. There was a point to this call and I could tell she was anxious to get there but was uncertain how to bring it up. Therefore, I could only assume that this movie she was asking about had something to do with coming home from Christmas. I mean, come on! My Last Christmas? Seriously?

I started to feel guilty about acting so gruff with my mother so I decided to humor her and ask a few questions about her movie.

"What channel was this movie on?" I asked. "I don't get too many channels out here but at least it's better than nothing. Maybe I have the channel."

My mother's face visibly brightened.

"It was on the new Greeting Card Network. They have been playing wholesome movies every night this week. It's part of their 'Home for the Holidays' gimmick they've been advertising."

Home for the holidays. I knew it. I braced for the worst.

"Speaking about that, can I ask you what you've decided to do for this Christmas?" my mother asked. "Are you going to come back here at least for Christmas? You can bring your new girlfriend. We'd love to meet her."

I took several deep calming breaths. As much as I wanted to tell my mother to mind her own business, I knew she was just doing what she thought needed to be done. I couldn't begrudge her for that.

"We've already talked about this, Mom," I reminded her. "Yesterday, in fact. You asked if I was planning on coming back there for Christmas. I can't. It's too soon. Everything reminds me of Samantha. I just assumed you would understand."

My mother suddenly smiled at me. I frowned. The hairs on the back of my neck suddenly stood up. She was up to something.

"I never would have imagined that living in that little Oregon town would mean so much to you," my mother admitted.

"I'm here because of Sam. I have this house and this winery because of her. I'm keeping the winery running in her honor. I think she'd like that."

"What does your new girlfriend say about that?" my mother asked.

"First off, she's not my girlfriend," I told my mother. "We had only just recently agreed to start seeing each other. We're not at the boyfriend/girlfriend stage yet."

"You always were touchy on that subject," my mother observed with a smile. "So can you tell me what you like most about that town? What was it called again? Pomme Valley?"

"That's right."

"What is it about Pomme Valley that you feel is better than Phoenix? We have all the modern conveniences of a big city..."

"...with the crime to match," I finished for her. "I'll be honest with you. I never would have thought I'd enjoy living in such a small town, but it has grown on me. The people here are nice. They look out for one another. I truly feel happy here. I can see myself settling down here. I can only hope that you'll let this particular matter drop. I don't want to have to keep defending myself to you. Will you do that for me?"

Surprisingly, my mother nodded.

"I only want you to be happy, Zachary. I... what was that?"

I had just made it to the house and walked inside. Puzzled, I looked down at her. I still thought this was a weird way to talk to someone, but you know what? It was actually nice to see her smiling up at me. Now, however, she was frowning at me.

"What was what, Mom? What's the matter?"

"I just saw something. When you held the phone up, presumably when you were opening your front door, I caught sight of something. Something orange. What was it?"

I smiled as I walked into my living room. I sat down on the couch and looked over at Watson. The little orange and white corgi had just circled a few times before stretching out on the floor in her customary 'flying squirrel' position. I held the phone up and turned it around, pointing the camera in Watson's direction.

"What is that?" I heard my mother ask. "Is that a small, orange, bearskin rug?"

I laughed and kept the phone pointed at Watson.

"I've never heard her referred to as a rug before. Watson!"

Watson's head jerked up off the floor. Her tongue flopped out and she panted contentedly. That's one of the things I like about corgis. They always looked like they were smiling at me. Watson watched me for a few moments before settling back to the floor.

"Is that a dog?" my mother asked.

I turned the phone back around and smiled at her.

"That was Watson. And yes, Watson is a dog."

"You have a dog now?" I heard my mother ask. I could actually hear her approval in the tone of her voice.

"I have two dogs," I corrected.

"Two dogs? Really? You've never owned a dog before. Why get two now?"

"Long story short, I was suckered into adopting Sherlock the first day I arrived here."

I heard the approaching clicks of doggie toenails on a tiled floor. Sherlock, upon hearing his name, had woken up from his nap on my bed, back in the master bedroom, and had come investigating. I turned the phone back around.

"Mom, this is Sherlock."

"Sherlock and Watson. Those are good names for dogs."

"Thanks. I thought so, too."

"So much has changed for you, Zachary."

"It's for the best, I assure you," I told my mother. "I needed a change, Mom. I'm now living in a place where I have more time to write, and most importantly, I am inspired to write. I have two dogs whom I think the world of, have reconnected with a friend I haven't seen since high school, and have since started a relationship with a very nice lady who has lived here in this town her entire life.

"This town is something else, Mom. Everyone is so nice. They've got this three month long festival still going on. Cider Fest. All the farms are selling fresh fruit, baked goods, and all manner of things. The town has been decorated with old-fashioned Christmas lights and I swear, if it snows here, we're going to see people riding around in horse-drawn sleighs."

"It sounds wonderful, Zachary. You sound happy."

"I am happy, Mom. For the first time since I can remember, I truly feel like I belong here."

"Well, you're right about one thing."

"What's that?"

"There's definitely more crime here in the Phoenix metropolitan area. I can only assume you have nothing like that in Pomme Valley."

Oops. No crime here? What was I supposed to tell her, that I somehow managed to bring the crime with me? Since I've been in town, Pomme Valley has had several murders and a high-profile theft.

Better leave that for another time.

"Now can you see why I don't want to go back to Phoenix for Christmas?" I asked. "Now do you see why I want to stay here? On top of which, it's awful hard to travel that far with two dogs."

"I understand, Zachary. I really do."

"Thank you. Will you at least stop asking me now? You're really making me feel bad every time I have to turn you down."

My mother suddenly smiled at me, as if she had just made up her mind about something. The hairs on the back of my neck jumped up. Again. Why did I get the feeling that I just shot myself in the foot?

"Very well. Since you won't be able to come to us for Christmas then we'll bring Christmas to you. It's settled. We'll see you in a few weeks."

Her picture disappeared and my phone reverted to its inert state. I remained, motionless, standing in the middle of my living room. I slowly looked down at the dogs.

"I should have kept my big mouth shut."

FOUR

You have no idea what she's like. I mean, she looks like a harmless little old lady, but man alive, can she lay on the guilt trip. I'm telling you, she has the power to twist a conversation around and make me out to be the world's worst son in less time than it takes to say, 'I told you so'."

Jillian stifled a giggle, "She couldn't possibly be that bad, Zachary. Don't you think it's possible that you might be over exaggerating? Just a little? This is your mother we're talking about."

Jillian and I were enjoying a nice lunch the following Monday, out on one of the many pet friendly terraces that looked out onto Main Street. Before you ask, yes, we were at Casa de Joe's. Don't judge. Anyway, Watson was snoozing by Jillian's feet while Sherlock entertained himself watching the general public pass by on the other side of the terrace. He was resting on the ground, Sphinx-like, next to my feet.

"Me? Over exaggerate? Perish the thought, woman."

"They're your family, Zachary. No matter how poorly you get along with them, they're still there for you. You should be proud of all that you've accomplished here in Pomme Valley. You're a successful business owner. You inherited PV's favorite winery, plus, you're the PVPD's secret weapon for solving crimes. What's not to love?"

"Maybe I am being a little too hard on them," I admitted. "After all, they didn't even know that I had two dogs living with me."

Surprised, Jillian returned her glass of iced tea to the table before she could take a sip.

"They don't know you have two corgis? Why didn't you tell them?"

"Ummm…"

"How often do you talk to your family, Zachary?" Jillian asked. A frown had settled over her lovely features and made me want to squirm in my seat.

"Oh, every so often."

"How long?"

"You know how it goes. Probably not nearly as much as I should."

"When was the last time you spoke with them?" Jillian asked, refusing to let the matter drop.

Hoo, boy. She wasn't going to like my answer. I was pretty sure I hadn't talked to either of my parents since I moved out here. We communicated via emails and texts, sure, but an actual conversation? Yesterday's video chat was the first time I've seen my mother in over six months.

Yeah, maybe I did deserve the title of World's Worst Kid.

"Let me try to put this another way. Does your family even know that you were arrested for murder?"

"If I say no, then are you going to think less of me?"

"Zachary Anderson! That's no way to treat your family. Were you serious when you insinuated that you and your parents don't get along? Is that why you didn't tell them that you had been arrested?"

"We've had our differences," I slowly began as the waitress appeared and set down our orders. I immediately started digging into my carne asada enchilada. "I think the reason I cringe whenever my mother calls is that it's because she still thinks of me as a teenager incapable of making my own decisions. I mean, I can appreciate her concern, but she really needs to let me make my own choices."

"Have you told her that?" Jillian asked.

"On numerous occasions. I just don't think it has ever sunk in."

"Then this would be the perfect opportunity to do just that," Jillian told me.

The waitress stopped by to refill our drinks. She caught sight of the two dogs and immediately put her tray down on our table. She squatted down and held out a hand. Recognizing a friendly gesture, both corgis rose to their feet and sniffed her hand.

"These have got to be the cutest dogs I've ever seen in my life!" the young waitress exclaimed.

Her name tag identified her as "Kim." She looked to be fresh out of high school, wore her long brunette hair in a tight braid, and had several visible tattoos. I'm not sure how long she's worked at Casa de Joe's, but I do know she's waited on us before.

Both dogs were gazing up at the young girl with adoring eyes as she first scratched Sherlock behind his ears and then gave Watson the same treatment. I was actually surprised Watson didn't flop over onto her back. I watched our waitress give her apron pockets a few pats, as if she was looking for something. She looked up at the two of us and smiled.

"I'll be right back. Is it okay if I give your dogs a treat?"

"As long as it isn't people food," I told her.

"They're these bits of bagel dough," Kim explained. "They're from…"

"I know exactly where you're going with this," I interrupted, giving her a smile. "And I can tell you that they both love those bagel bit things from Farmhouse Bakery."

"Awesome! I'll be right back!"

"You've made a friend," Jillian giggled.

I shook my head and pointed at the dogs.

"You mean they have. Everywhere I go people ooh and aah over the dogs. As for me? I'm ignored."

"Unless you identify yourself," Jillian added with a smile. "You're quite the celebrity around here, Zachary."

I shrugged. "Not for the right reasons."

My cell started to ring. I glanced at the display and groaned. I showed Jillian the phone. It was Vance.

"Do you know what I'm going to do?" I asked her. "I'm going to see about changing his ring tone to 'You're a mean one, Mr. Grinch.' That'd fit him quite well right about now."

Jillian shook her head. "No, you're not. He's your friend. Just answer it and see what he wants. Hopefully everything is okay."

Unfortunately, it wasn't.

"Zack. Did I catch you at a bad time?"

Kim appeared just then, fed each of the corgis a couple

treats, and presented me with the check. I signaled her to wait and slid a credit card into the small black binder, all without looking at the bill. She smiled, nodded, and hurried off.

"We're just finishing up lunch. What's going on? You don't sound like you're having a good day."

"I'm not. There's been another burglary."

I sighed and looked over at Jillian. She was already watching me and knew instantly that something was wrong.

"Another burglary," I quietly whispered to her.

"Same as before. All the presents are gone and there are no signs of forced entry. There's definitely something going on here since this house is much nicer and there are all kinds of things that would tempt a burglar."

"Only nothing else was taken," I quietly guessed.

"Right. I don't suppose you have the dogs with you, do you?"

"As a matter of fact, they're right here."

"Oh, good. Come on down here. The address is…"

"So is Jillian," I added, perhaps a wee bit more forcefully than I should have.

"Oh. My bad. I'm sorry, Zack. I should've asked. I can just…"

Jillian took the phone from me, "Don't worry, Vance. I'm sending him your way."

I stared at Jillian with a bemused smile on my face. Yes, she could have guessed at how the conversation was playing out, but to grab the phone at the right time? Could she have heard him? Darn women and their Vulcan hearing.

Jillian pulled out a piece of paper and pen and jotted down an address. She finished the call and handed me the phone. Then she slid the paper over to me.

"Better get going. He's expecting you."

"I'm not sure how much help we'll be able to be," I confided, as we both pushed our chairs back. "Sherlock didn't find anything at the first place."

"Maybe he will with this one," Jillian suggested. "You never know. It's worth a shot, right?"

I dropped Jillian off at Cookbook Nook and headed over to the second crime scene. This one was located in a nicer, newer part of town. I parked my Jeep just off of Blackstone Alley and set both Sherlock and Watson on the ground. Together we headed toward all the flashing lights and bustle of activity. This time I could see an elderly couple being interviewed by the police. I looked up at the house. Vance was right. This was definitely a nicer part of town.

The house was a contemporary two-story home that had an attached two car garage. The grounds were professionally landscaped, as were the rest of the properties on this street. A quick glance down the street confirmed that each and every single house had been decorated for Christmas. Maybe it was part of some HOA agreement. Whatever. I will say that it looked really nice. I headed toward the open front door. I could see Vance standing inside, talking with the same crime scene tech I had seen him with yesterday. As before, we were waved over.

"This is a nice place," I commented, as the dogs and I stepped foot inside. I could smell the telltale scent of freshly cut pine trees coming from within. I could also smell cleaning supplies. This house had been recently cleaned. A quick glance at the carpet showed that it had been recently vacuumed, too.

"Zack. Thanks for coming. Well, here we are again."

"This place is a lot nicer than the last," I observed. "It's beautiful in here. Makes me realize I haven't decorated for Christmas at my house. Yet."

Vance nodded. "Better get with it. Christmas is two weeks away. Yep, this place is more upscale than the last. That's what makes this even more baffling. This house has a top-notch home theater system. The homeowners have a jewelry box inside their walk-in closet. They even have a floor safe. Nothing was touched, only the presents. It doesn't even seem like they were looking for anything besides the presents."

"What kinds of presents were there?" I asked. "Anything worth a lot of bucks?"

"Just presents for their grandkids. Various toys, a few electronic games, tablets, etc. Don't get me wrong, they're worth more than what the Murphy family had, but still, look at this room! That's gotta be a what, 55- or 60-inch flat screen TV, with a top of the line home theater system. The speakers alone are probably worth just as much as the television, yet they were ignored. What kind of an idiotic burglar would do that?"

"Somebody who's looking for a very specific item," I decided. "What that could be escapes me at the moment."

"That makes two of us," Vance confessed.

"So who lives here?" I asked.

"Dr. and Mrs. David Morris."

"Doctor, huh?"

Vance nodded. "He's retired."

"Maybe we're dealing with a disgruntled former patient?"

"He was a dentist," Vance pointed out. "What, did someone not like their cleaning?"

"I take it they didn't see or hear anything?"

Vance shook his head. "Nope. Not a thing. They stepped out for lunch and when they came back, they were shocked to see everything was missing from under their tree."

"No open windows or unlocked back doors?" I asked.

"None. We've been over every square inch of this house. It was locked up tighter than a drum."

"So how is this guy finding a way in?" I demanded. "Look, I'm no expert, but I'd say we're definitely missing something. No broken windows, unlocked doors, or ... what about hidden keys?"

Vance turned to look at me.

"What was that?"

"Did the good doctor have a house key hidden somewhere around here? Maybe under a planter or a rock?"

Surprised, Vance motioned one of the officers over and relayed the question. The officer hurried over to the retired doctor and asked. We both saw the doctor turn our way and shake his head no.

"So much for that."

"It was a good idea," Vance told me. "I'm surprised I hadn't thought of that."

"I should've known it wouldn't have panned out. I mean, the first burglary was an apartment. There's not many places to hide a key there."

"A valid point," Vance admitted.

"If I didn't know any better, then I'd say a pissed off Santa Claus was reclaiming gifts."

An officer approached. He was an officer I was familiar with, but sadly, his name escaped me. He held a notebook out to Vance.

"What's this?" he asked the officer.

"A more detailed list of what was under the tree."

Vance turned to look at me.

"Alright. You're here. So are Sherlock and Watson. Care to lead them around to see if they spot anything while I go through this?"

"You got it. Sherlock, let's go. Let's see if there's anything to find in here, okay?"

Sherlock was waiting. As soon as he felt slack appear in his leash he was on his feet and headed farther into the house. He sniffed along the perimeter of the living room— again, hesitating at the tree—and promptly moved toward the kitchen.

We checked out the bathrooms. We checked the bedrooms, the den, and the laundry room. I walked both dogs through the garage just to see if anything attracted Sherlock's attention.

Nothing.

Every time I asked the little fellow if there was anything here, he always returned to the tree to stare up at it, as though he had never laid eyes on a tree before in his life. Determined to figure out what he was so fascinated with, I squatted down next to Sherlock and together we stared at the tree. Watson joined us a few moments later; only after a second or two, she was staring at me as though I had finally lost my marbles.

"Whatcha got?" Vance asked, as he squatted down next to me.

"This is the second tree that Sherlock has expressed interest in," I told Vance. "Coincidence? And before you ask, yes, he has seen a tree before."

"Weren't you the one who said that Sherlock's

fascination with the tree could be attributed to the simple fact that he's never seen one indoors before?"

"Yeah, I did. However, here we are, at two crime scenes in a row, and Sherlock has got his nose in the tree again. Isn't it worth checking out?"

Vance slowly stood. It was nice to see that his knees cracked just as loudly going up as mine did going down. We both eyed each other and decided to refrain from cracking a joke at the other's expense.

"I'd be more interested in knowing whether it's all indoor Christmas trees Sherlock is interested in or just these two. Then I'd be willing to check out the tree. But until that happens, I think we can leave the tree alone."

I gathered up the leashes and headed outside.

"That's easy enough to test out," I told my friend as we made it to the sidewalk.

"Oh, yeah?" Vance countered. "How?"

"Look at all the bystanders out here," I said, indicating the growing crowd of curious onlookers. "Do you think we could persuade one of them to let us in to check out their tree?"

"Honey, you can come in my house any time you want."

I groaned. Unfortunately, the voice was one that I knew. It belonged to Ms. Clara Hanson, owner of PV's only bookstore, A Lazy Afternoon. I had met her a few months ago when I went looking for books about Egyptian mummies. This was the lady who, I was certain, was smack in the middle of a mid-life crisis. She was doing her damnedest to try and reclaim her youth by dressing in skin-tight clothes and showing way more skin than anyone wanted to see. She acted like she was a teenager, only the problem was, she had to be in her sixties. The last time I saw her—which was the day we met—her hair was a bright platinum blond skyscraper that was perching precariously on her head. I thought it had to be a wig, but never had enough guts to ask about it. Today, though, she was a brunette and her ~~jet black~~ brown locks were straight as an arrow and extended halfway down her back.

I groaned.

Ever since the day I met her I have been actively avoiding her. I'm not afraid of little old ladies, don't get me wrong. However, I'm not a fan of people who don't respect my private space. I don't like carrying on conversations with anyone who was determined to hold them less than two inches from my face.

Both dogs had already turned at the sound of the voice and were watching the stranger closely. Vance turned and looked, having heard me groan. He nudged my shoulder.

"A fan of yours?"

"Unfortunately. Man, I gotta tell you, she scares the bejeezus out of me."

"Her? Why?"

"Let's just say that she's a little on the too-friendly side."

"Ah. Still want to try this experiment of yours?"

"Not now I don't."

Much to my dismay, Vance turned to Ms. Hanson and waved her over. Clara couldn't duck under the yellow tape and hurry over to us fast enough. I threw Vance a dirty look.

"Well, hello there, boys! I couldn't help but overhear your conversation. You're looking for a house with a Christmas tree in it? Well, mine's right next door. You're more than welcome to come inside and look around. Hello again, Zack! It's so nice to see you, sweetie."

"Umm…"

Vance held out a hand.

"Vance Samuelson, PVPD. And who might you be, ma'am?"

Clara took the hand and gave it a firm shake.

"Clara Hanson. I own A Lazy Afternoon, off of Oregon Street."

Vance nodded. "The bookstore. I've been to your store a few times, ma'am. Zack and I are curious and want to see if his dogs react strangely to all indoor trees."

"Sure thing, honey. Come this way. I'd enjoy the company of such handsome men."

Thankfully, since I was standing several feet behind my friend, Clara slipped her arm through Vance's and pulled him toward her house first. I followed from a discreet distance. I glanced down at the dogs to see what their reaction to this pushy woman was. From what I could see, neither one appeared to care.

We walked up the steps to Clara's home, pausing only long enough for the homeowner to open her front door. A waft of incense, oils, and a myriad of other nauseating scents wafted out, nearly making me gag. This was almost as bad as walking into a smoker's home. I could only hope my clothes weren't going to smell like this for the rest of the day.

"Zack, see if Sherlock is interested in this tree. It's right over there."

I narrowed my eyes. I could see that Vance's eyes were watering. Clearly, he was enjoying his time inside Clara's house just as much as I was.

I led Sherlock over to the living room, gave him some slack, and silently watched to see what he'd do. Watson promptly sat by my right ankle and watched her packmate. Sure enough, as soon as Sherlock neared the tree, his ears perked up and he gazed up at it with the same amount of fascination as he'd exhibited with the other two.

So much for that theory. My crackpot dog was apparently fascinated with indoor trees. There was nothing more to learn here, so it was time to beat a hasty retreat. I gathered up his leash and led him back to the front door.

"He's acting the same way," I confirmed. "You were right, Vance. It's just a passing fancy. We should get going."

"Give us a kiss, give us a kiss."

Both Vance and I turned at the sound of a second voice. I smiled at Vance's confusion. He thought there was someone else in the house.

"It's her parrot," I told him. "Ruby, if memory serves."

I heard a flapping of wings and then, all of a sudden, I felt something perch on my right shoulder. A soft, feathered head nuzzled up against my cheek.

"Do you know this bird, Zack?" Vance asked.

I nodded. "Kinda. I've only seen her once before, in Clara's store."

Ruby cooed softly, trilling quietly every few seconds.

"I have never seen her do that," Clara admitted. "She doesn't even do that with me. What's she doing? The bird equivalent of a purr?"

I looked at Clara and shrugged. "I'm no ornithologist. I haven't a clue."

"Ornithologist?" Vance repeated.

"A bird expert," I translated.

We all heard a few warning woofs. Sherlock, with his neck craned all the way up to look at me, was eyeing the gray parrot. He woofed again. I saw Ruby stop her nuzzling, look down at the two dogs who were staring up at her, and then bob her head a few times.

"Give us a kiss, Precious. Give us a kiss."

Sherlock fired off another warning woof. Apparently, he didn't feel comfortable with his daddy having a bird perched on his shoulder. What happened next had me gasping with surprise and alarm.

Ruby flew off my shoulder and landed ... on Sherlock's rump.

"Oh, snap," I muttered.

Sherlock's head started to turn. His neck slowly twisted until he was looking straight at the small parrot that was perched on his butt. There was a pregnant pause as I sucked in a breath. What was Sherlock going to do?

I was reminded of an afternoon I had spent at Turf Paradise, a horse racing track in Phoenix. Everyone would wait, with baited breath, for the gates to open and horses to take off. Well, that's what he had here, only this time we had a single rider.

Sherlock took off like a bat out of hell. The leashes were pulled from my grip. I hastily retrieved Watson's before she could bolt, too.

I have to hand it to Ruby. That little parrot was one heck of a rider. The African gray parrot had partially extended her wings for balance but she managed to stay upright on Sherlock's back.

Sherlock zoomed by us on his way to the kitchen. Ruby cackled with delight. The corgi literally spun around on Clara's tiled kitchen floor and sprinted back by us. Ruby was doing her head-bobbing thing as they went by a second time.

Finally, after the fourth circuit through the house,

Sherlock made it back into the living room, checked his rear to see if he had dislodged his rider, and once he saw that he hadn't, did something that amazed me.

He dropped to the ground and rolled.

Before I could shout an order for Sherlock to stop—I didn't want Ruby to be hurt—I caught myself yet again. Ruby apparently had another skillset besides being a bronco rider, and that was a being a log roller. The moment Sherlock hit the ground and rolled, Ruby waddled off his back and onto his stomach. Sherlock was on his feet in a flash. Ruby had already returned to her perch on his rump.

Sherlock gave me an exasperated look and again rolled. Once more, Ruby log-rolled the corgi and landed on his back as he rose to his feet. I burst out laughing, as did Vance and Clara.

"That is hands down the funniest thing I've ever seen," Clara squeezed out between laughs. "Just when you think you know your pet, she goes and does something like that!"

I walked toward Sherlock and noticed I got both bronco and rider's attention. On a whim, I tapped my shoulder and called to Ruby. Sure enough, the parrot flew to my shoulder and was back to nuzzling my face.

"You're a little on the creepy side, Dr. Doolittle," Vance quipped.

"You'd better take her," I told Clara. "I need to make certain Sherlock is okay."

Clara reached for Ruby, much to the parrot's dismay. The little parrot squawked in protest. Loudly. Once she was safely back inside her cage, I squatted down next to Sherlock.

"Are you okay, pal? You probably have never had a rider, huh?"

The look Sherlock threw me suggested he never wanted another and, should I disagree, I could go jump in front of a bus. I ruffled his fur and picked up his leash. Vance handed me Watson's and we turned for the door.

We thanked Clara for the use of her home, while steadfastly refusing her offer to stay for dinner. We both desperately needed fresh air. Once we were outside, I turned to Vance, made sure we weren't being watched, and shuddered.

And then shuddered again.

"It's too bad someone didn't record that," Vance lamented. "That could have gone viral on the internet. People pay big money to see that kind of thing."

"That parrot sure took to me," I recalled.

"Have you ever owned a parrot before?" Vance asked. "Maybe she could sense you were a bird lover?"

I shook my head. "Nope. Sherlock was the very first pet I've ever had, followed almost immediately by Watson."

"Clara Hanson sure is something," Vance decided.

"She creeps me out," I admitted.

"She certainly seems to like you," Vance said, with a smirk on his face. He gave me a grin. "So, tell me. Is she your type?"

I hit Vance on the arm. Hard.

FIVE

"Now what are you barking at?" I asked Sherlock as we pulled out of the library's parking lot on the west side of town.

I should back up just a moment. It was now Tuesday morning, a little past 10 a.m. I had just anonymously donated a stack of my books to the local library, to see if there might be any interest in them here in PV. As I was getting back in my Jeep, I noticed a vendor had set up shop selling Christmas trees in the far corner of the library's parking lot. A pickup truck, complete with a full-sized camper, was parked nearby. Curious to see how Sherlock would react, and also remembering that I still hadn't put up a single decoration back home, I purchased a tree.

Ever try to haul an oversized item in a vehicle with no

room to haul it? What a pain. I will be cleaning needles out of my Jeep for months to come, I'm sure. Thankfully, I could roll the back window of my Jeep down and stick the part of the tree that didn't fit through the opening. I had to laugh once I saw the result. It looked as though I had an unfortunate run-in with a tree while going in reverse. Down a hill.

Sherlock and Watson absolutely loved it. They knew something was up and kept rearing up on their hind legs to peer over the back seat. Thankfully I knew they couldn't get back there, but it was funny watching them try.

As soon as we had made it back to Main, traveling east, Sherlock and Watson finally tired of peering at the tree poking out of the back window and settled down on their seats. However, at the exact moment Sherlock curled up, he was suddenly back on his feet and barking for all he was worth. Naturally, Watson had to join him.

"What are you barking at?" I asked. We were driving down PV's busiest street, at the busiest time of day. There were cars, people, and all kinds of activities happening all around us. There was no way to tell what could have set the corgi off. "If there's something you'd like me to check out, then I don't suppose you could help me out and point at that at which you're barking? Whataya say?"

Surprisingly, Sherlock rushed over to the right side of the Jeep and thrust his nose out one of the small gaps I had left in either passenger window. He barked several times. Watson pushed her nose through, too, and also added her two cents.

I looked right. We were just passing Gary's Grocery and the demolition crew hard at work taking down the old Square L convenience store. All the same machines were still there and were presently in use. The backhoe was busy loading up the debris from the bulldozer, which was busy turning the store into a pancake. One dump truck was half full and the other was empty, awaiting its turn. The cargo van was also there, but parked farther away.

"I'll be glad when that place is gone," I said aloud, to no one in particular. "Then maybe I'll be able to drive by it without the dogs going ballistic. Sherlock? Care to give it a rest? There's nothing there to report, pal. It's just a demolition zone now, that's all."

Once we made it home, I unloaded the tree, tried to vacuum as many of the needles as I could from the back of my Jeep, and promptly gave up once I saw that somehow each needle must've super-glued itself to my Jeep's mats. I dug out the tree holder I had seen in the garage on more than one occasion and set the tree up in my living room, to the left of the fireplace.

There. Now, with a tree currently sitting indoors, in my own house, I was curious to see how Sherlock would react to it. I had left both corgis in the master bedroom and had closed the door during the setup process. Now that the tree was upright and inside the house, it was time to, if you'll pardon the pun, let the dogs out.

Sherlock trotted out of the room, headed straight to the living room, and gazed at the newest addition to the house decor. Then he promptly turned his back on the tree and ambled toward his basket of doggie toys. I stared at the tree for a few moments longer, half expecting Sherlock to return to it for a closer examination.

Nothing.

The little booger didn't have the slightest interest in the house's newest decoration. Nor did Watson, for that matter. Well, maybe the tree needed to be decorated. My predecessor must have had Christmas decorations somewhere around the house. Maybe in the attic? I certainly hadn't seen anything else in the garage.

My cell rang. It was Jillian.

"Hello, Zachary! Did I catch you at a bad time?"

"Not at all. As a matter of fact, I just put up a Christmas tree and was about ready to go on a scavenger hunt for some decorations. I figure old Aunt Bonnie must've had some ornaments somewhere around here."

"How very festive of you! Would you like some help?"

"You won't catch me turning down free help. I'd love some."

"Excellent! We'll be right over. See you in a few."

I looked at Sherlock and hooked a thumb toward the stairs.

"I have to go to the attic. Will you two be okay down here or would you like to…"

Sherlock trotted off before I had time to finish my sentence. He glanced at Watson as he passed her and walked toward the stairs. After a second's worth of hesitation, Watson joined him. I found the two of them waiting patiently at the foot of the stairs. Once I had carried each of them up the flight of steps, we headed to the bedroom with the attic access in the closet.

"I won't be long," I told the dogs. "Wait for me."

Tucked away in a far corner of the attic, I hit the proverbial jackpot. I found over a dozen boxes all labeled 'Xmas Decorations' in a neat scrawl written across the top. I took at least half a dozen of the boxes down the attic stairs when it hit me. Jillian had said we'll. So who else was she bringing over? It's not like her to pull any surprises on me.

I hurriedly carried the dogs back down to the first floor and then brought my boxes down. A quick check of the house had me cringing. I had little bits of trash and dirty dishes all over the coffee table and I could see that I hadn't tidied up the kitchen since … since … well, probably since the last time I had Jillian over.

The next fifteen minutes disappeared in the blink of an eye. The kitchen was cleaned. The dishwasher was unloaded. I even took the trash out. Satisfied with the house's current condition, I returned to the living room and, in a rare moment of inspiration, turned on the TV and set the channel to one of those digital audio channels. I heard a car pull up outside just as Bing Crosby began crooning about white Christmases. It had to be Jillian.

I started toward the door when I heard three distinctive thuds as three separate car doors were slammed shut. I looked down at Sherlock. By this time both corgis were staring at the front door, having heard the car approach as well.

I held up a finger. "No. No barking. They're guests, okay?"

I heard Jillian knock. She never seemed to enjoy ringing the doorbell. Sherlock started with his warning woofs. Watson stared at her packmate, as if to say that she was okay with whatever course of action he deemed to choose.

I opened the door and was surprised to see Jillian, Hannah, and a young boy I had never seen before. This had to be Colin, Hannah's son. Both Hannah and the boy appeared to be quiet and withdrawn. I groaned silently. Something must have happened with Hannah's jerk of a husband. I looked at Jillian and opened my mouth to ask a question when she quickly shook her head no. Her eyes met mine and I could see that they were pleading with me to be okay with this. I gave her a slight nod. I opened the door as wide as it could and gave my guests what I hoped was a welcoming smile.

"Hey there! Come in! It's cold out there." A few woofs sounded from behind me. "Sherlock, Watson, come here."

Two corgis appeared by my side, as if they had been waiting for me to issue that particular command.

"Guys, we have some guests. This is ... Sherlock? Stop woofing. They're friends. Hello, Hannah." I looked at the boy and offered him a friendly smile. I held out a hand. "You're Colin, right?"

The boy sullenly nodded. He gave me a lackluster hand shake.

"Hannah, Colin, bear with me. I need to make introductions or else I'm going to have a canine mutiny on my hands. Guys, this is Sherlock and Watson."

Both corgis craned their necks to look up at our two guests. Sherlock looked at Hannah, whined, and raised a paw, as if he wanted to shake hands with her. Hannah smiled fleetingly at the dogs and gave each one a pat on the head. Colin seemed to perk up the moment he noticed four sets of canine eyes now watching him.

"Can I pet your dogs?" the boy timidly asked.

I nodded. "Sure. But, I should warn you about something."

Alarmed, Colin looked up at me.

"What?"

"If you pet them, or pay any amount of attention to them, they won't leave you alone as long as you're in this house."

The boy smiled at that. I ushered him into the living room, gestured for him to take a seat on the floor, and waited for everyone else to sit down. Jillian, who knew what was coming, stifled a giggle.

"What is it?" I heard Hannah ask in a hushed voice. "What's the matter?"

"Colin likes dogs, right?" Jillian asked.

Hannah nodded. "Yes. Why?"

"Watch this. Okay, Zachary. You can release the hounds."

Both corgis were watching me. Waiting. I grinned and squatted down to drape an arm around each of them.

"Are you ready?" I asked them.

"Awwooooo!" Sherlock howled. He only had eyes for the boy.

Watson was wriggling. Kinda. She was in the process of doing this slo-mo crawl across the carpet, all without breaking her 'down'. I looked over at Colin and grinned at him.

"Ready to be properly introduced, corgi style?"

"Uh, sure?"

"Okay, guys. Go get him."

By the time I said 'him', both corgis had launched themselves at the boy and had knocked him over onto his back. Sherlock had draped himself across Colin's chest— as though he was afraid he'd get away—and was licking the boy's face with well-timed licks. Watson was barking excitedly and was darting in every time Colin, in an effort to get away from Sherlock's long tongue, would look her way. Then he'd get another kiss on a different part of his face.

"Ack-Pbttth! What the… Geez, these dogs are strong!"

However, no one could mistake the laughter or the joy which was emanating from Hannah's son. He was smiling, giggling uncontrollably, and rolling around on the floor while both corgis circled him like lions circling their kill.

The dogs loved it.

"We needed this," I heard Hannah confidentially tell Jillian in a hushed tone. "Thank you."

"Don't thank me, thank Zachary," Jillian said.

I let Colin suffer under the corgi-attack for another minute or two before I called them off. Colin sat up and wiped his mouth with the back of an arm. He looked over at the dogs, smiled, and then twisted around to look at his mother sitting nearby.

"Mom, do you think we could get a dog? One like that?" he finished, pointing at Sherlock.

"We'll see, sweetheart," Hannah told the boy. "We'll see."

I clapped my hands together and stood up.

"Okay, look at all the slave labor I have at my disposal."

Hannah smiled at me and nodded.

"We're here, ready to help. Put us to work."

I pointed at the boxes I had brought down and then I pointed at the tree.

"I'm looking for decorations to put on the tree. I figure they've got to be in there somewhere. Feel free to go through those boxes and see if there's anything good in any of them. There's probably half a dozen other boxes in the attic, waiting to come down. I'll go get them."

By the time I had the rest of the Christmas boxes sitting in the living room, along with a few others I found after conducting a thorough search of the rest of the house's closets, I had nearly two dozen dusty boxes of various sizes sitting inside my living room. Jillian and Hannah were slowly and methodically going through the boxes, while

Colin kept the dogs entertained.

Turns out Aunt Bonnie really enjoyed decorating. It also looked as though Bonnie must've either been part Scandinavian or else she really enjoyed red and white decorations. Blankets, trinkets, candy dishes, rugs, tree skirts, and all manner of bric-a-brac were there.

"So how would you like to do this?" Jillian asked me.

"If you're asking how I'd like things decorated," I began, "then I can say that I haven't a clue. I wouldn't say no to some creative input."

Jillian opened another box and pulled out a large red table cloth with white snowflakes all over it. She automatically moved toward the oak dining table. Hannah began clearing it.

"Do I have free reign to decorate how I'd like?" Jillian asked.

"Have at it," I assured her. "I like how you've decorated your store and your house. Feel free to work your magic in here."

Several hours later it looked as though Christmas had blown up in my house. While a few of the decorations found their way to other parts of the house, the vast majority of the decorations were in the living room. After finding a box of carefully packed hand-blown glass ornaments, the ladies had decorated the tree with care.

Even Colin helped. I appointed him duly-designated master of candy canes. Every time I checked on his progress, he had a piece of candy cane sticking out of his mouth. I had to assure Hannah, after she pulled me aside, that I had picked up a box of candy canes the other day and he was more than welcome to the whole thing if he wanted.

A solid red tree skirt, trimmed with faux white fur, had been placed beneath the tree. The lights, I noticed with dismay, were the old fashioned C7 bulbs. I hadn't seen bulbs that size since I was a kid back in the early '80s. Next year, I'd replace them with the much more cost-efficient LED strands.

Several red and white throws had been placed on the backs of the couches. Even the pictures on the walls looked as though they had been replaced because everywhere I looked I could see scenes of horse-drawn sleighs crossing snowy hills. The picture above the fireplace was of an idyllic Dickensian village, complete with cobblestone streets, horse drawn carriages, and gas-powered street lights.

I moved closer to the picture and squinted at it. Yes, that sign over one of the business doors clearly said 'Marley & Scrooge, with a big 'X' over Marley's name. It was right out of Charles Dickens' A Christmas Carol. How cool!

"Where'd you find this?" I asked as I turned to Jillian.

"Front closet," she informed me. "That's where all these pictures and paintings came from. You have quite a collection in there. I didn't even use half of them."

"That closet isn't that big," I protested. "There's no way I could have missed seeing it."

"There's a storage bay just inside the closet," Hannah helpfully supplied. "I almost missed it myself. I was hanging up my jacket when I saw it."

"Zachary? Would you give me a hand in the kitchen for just a second?"

I looked up in time to see Jillian walk around the corner into the kitchen.

"Sure."

"Thank you so much for going along with this," Jillian

whispered to me as soon as I came around the corner.

"Hey, no problem," I whispered back. "What's going on? Is everything okay with Hannah?"

"Is everything okay in there?" Hannah called from the front room. "Do you need any help with anything?"

Thinking quickly, I smiled. I pulled out my cell.

"What kind of pizza do you and Colin like? You guys have been such a tremendous help that pizza is on me tonight. What kind would you like?"

Hannah appeared.

"Oh, you don't have to do that. Not on our account."

I gave Hannah a neutral stare.

"Hey, Colin?"

The boy appeared.

"Yes?"

"What's your favorite pizza?"

"Pepperoni!"

I winked at the kid, "Now we're talking. Nice to meet someone else with awesome taste buds. What type does your mother like?"

Colin made a face. "She likes those kinds with all the gunk in them. I wouldn't touch them with a ten foot pole."

I laughed. "Let me guess. She likes combination pizzas?"

Colin nodded. "Right."

I cast a glance at Hannah to confirm. She sighed and nodded her head. I looked at Jillian.

"Are you good with those?"

"I love combination pizzas," Jillian said.

"And you two are more than welcome to 'em. Colin and I will have pepperoni, thank you very much." I gave the boy a high five.

The pizza was ordered. It arrived a half hour later. Sated, I sat back on the couch and watched Colin play with the dogs. Sherlock disappeared behind a recliner and reemerged with a tennis ball in his mouth. He gave a muffled bark and spit the ball at Colin's feet. In moments both corgis were barking joyously at the bouncing ball and going ballistic every time it was thrown.

"I never knew such small dogs had such loud barks," Hannah observed.

"I've told Zachary that corgis are essentially big dogs wrapped up in small dog packages," Jillian said.

Hannah laughed. "What an apt description!"

I had just taken a long pull on my beer when the topic of conversation turned dark.

"So are you going to be okay?" Jillian asked as she turned toward Hannah.

Both were sitting on the couch with me. I was on Jillian's left while Hannah was on her right. I tapped Jillian on her shoulder.

"Would you like me to leave for this?"

Hannah shook her head. "No. Zack, please stay. I think I'd like a man's opinion here." She took another swig from her own beer before she continued. Her voice dropped so that her son couldn't overhear her. "As you have no doubt noticed, you're not catching Colin and me at our best."

"I gathered as much," I said. "Are you and Colin okay?"

Hannah nodded. "We will be." She sighed. "Where to start. Well, I guess it would have started early this morning."

"What happened this morning?" Jillian wanted to know.

"Dylan and I got into a huge fight."

"About what?" Jillian asked.

"He told me that he was going out of town."

Jillian groaned. "He does that all the time. You'd think he'd want to spend more time with you and Colin."

"He's going to be gone over Christmas," Hannah quietly added. She pulled a tissue from her purse and dabbed at the corners of her eyes. "If you could've seen the look on Colin's face when his father broke the news to him. It was devastating. It broke my heart."

"Then why is the jerk ditching his family on a major holiday?" I asked in a low voice. "What kind of moron does that?"

Both women turned to regard me as though I was the dumbest thing on two legs.

"What? Why are you looking at me like that?"

"I suspect Dylan is having an affair," Hannah said miserably.

Okay, maybe I was the dumbest thing on two legs. I should've seen that coming.

"You know my thoughts on this matter," Jillian matter-of-factly said.

Hannah nodded. "I do. Zack? What's your take on all of this?"

I set my beer down on the coffee table and was silent as I considered. I stared into the depths of my bottle as I searched for the proper thing to say. After a few minutes had passed I cleared my throat.

"Not everyone appreciates—or understands—what being a family is all about," I slowly began. "I don't know if I'm the right one to ask about this particular subject, but I will tell you what I've discovered about myself." I was silent for another minute. "Families are supposed to spend their time together. They're supposed to want to be together, especially for the holidays. You're supposed to look forward to going home to see everyone, but do I? The answer is no. I'm ashamed to say that I've been pushing my family away ever since Samantha died. Talking about … about Sam's death is not something I enjoy doing."

"Then you certainly don't have to now," Hannah assured me. "I wouldn't want to…"

"It's okay," I interrupted. "The point I was trying to make is that ever since Samantha died, I've noticed I've been pushing my family away, even though I'm sure they're only trying to help. What other son would scowl every time his mother calls?"

"Why do you think you've been pushing them away?" Jillian softly asked.

"I don't know. I guess I'm afraid of facing them. Since Samantha died, I've only seen them once, and that was at her funeral. I haven't really talked to them about this and I know I should. It's just that I feel so guilty."

"Guilty about what?" Hannah wanted to know.

Just then a yellow tennis ball bounced by us with two corgis in hot pursuit. Colin appeared. He was sprinting after them, laughing hysterically. They hit the tile in the front entry and went skidding out of sight. We could all hear maniacal barking and a mad scrambling as both dogs struggled to stay in pursuit of the ball.

I shook my head. "Dogs. You asked what I had to feel guilty about. That's easy. Sam's death. She told me she had errands to run. If only I had gone with her, then she might still be alive."

"Or the both of you could be dead," Jillian observed. "There's no point in second-guessing yourself, Zachary. There's nothing you could've done except possibly get yourself killed, too."

"If you don't mind me asking," Hannah hesitantly said, "could you tell me how she died?"

"Car accident," I answered. I took a deep breath and polished off my beer.

"Bad weather?" Hannah asked.

I shook my head. "It was Phoenix. It was sunny. The only conclusion I was ever given was that Samantha lost control of her car and it veered out into oncoming traffic. She was hit head-on by a semi. Thankfully she died instantly."

"Jillian's right," Hannah said, nodding her head. "There's absolutely nothing you could have done. Whether or not you were driving was irrelevant. The car malfunctioned and it swerved out into traffic. It's not your fault."

"You may be right," I told the girls. "It still hurts, though. So, since I took the long road around to answer your question, I'd like to think a man wouldn't willingly abandon his wife and child on Christmas unless there was a super good reason."

"Was there?" Jillian asked. "A reason, that is."

Hannah shook her head. "No. He never gave any explanation, only that he had someplace to be. And do you know what really hurts? He didn't act that upset about it. I think this confirms my suspicions. He must be having an affair. It's the only plausible explanation I can think of."

Hannah's eyes filled, which resulted in sympathetic tears from Jillian.

"I have no idea what we're going to do for Christmas now," Hannah continued. "I have no idea how I'm going to explain this to Colin. Even though Dylan is a jerk, I don't want to be home alone on Christmas."

"I had no idea things were that bad," Jillian whispered, pulling out yet another tissue from her purse. Seeing that Hannah could use a fresh tissue, too, she gave her friend hers and grabbed another for herself.

"I have the perfect solution," I announced.

Jillian and Hannah looked at me, askance.

"Come here. We'll have one big party. We'll have snacks, movies, and enough food to feed a…"

"And games?" Jillian asked, clapping her hands delightedly.

"Only if you agree to head up the entertainment department," I told her.

Jillian nodded. "Of course! Oh, this will be so much fun!"

"I wouldn't want to impose," Hannah began.

"Nonsense," I stated, waving off her concerns. "Jillian will be here. So will my parents, since they were unsuccessful in guilting me to return to Phoenix. You can help act as a buffer. I know I need to level with them, only I don't want to have to worry about this. Not just yet. Will you help me, Hannah?"

"And you don't mind having Colin run around here?" Hannah dubiously asked.

At that precise moment, a horizontal tornado tore by us, consisting of one laughing boy and two pursing corgis.

"Not at all," I assured her. "Colin can be our duly designated dog sitter."

"Thank you, Zachary," Hannah quietly said.

"We are going to have so much fun!" Jillian announced, pulling a small notebook and pen from her purse. "Now, let's get organized."

"What can I do?" Hannah asked. "You've got to let me do something."

While the two ladies plotted out the oncoming festivities, my thoughts turned to the string of burglaries that had befallen PV. Two families were going to have bleak Christmases, thanks to some thoughtless crook. I remembered the plans I had set in motion and smiled. Well, make that one family was going to be disappointed, and I'm fairly certain the retired doctor would be able to replace the missing gifts with other presents. It was the Murphy family who were the most in need.

Not this Christmas season, I mentally vowed. If only they knew what was in store for them.

"Penny for your thoughts."

I looked up and found Jillian's soft eyes gazing into my own.

"Nothing much. I was just thinking about the burglaries that happened in the last couple of days."

Jillian sighed. "Those poor families. Hopefully there weren't any small children involved."

"The second burglary was at the home of a retired doctor," I told the ladies. "While unfortunate, I'm sure he can afford to buy replacements."

"And the first?" Hannah whispered, certain she already knew the answer.

"It was an apartment in the northern part of town. They had two small kids, a boy and a girl."

"Oh, no," Jillian gasped. "I think I know the apartments you're talking about. If they're living there then they probably don't..."

"They don't," I confirmed, cutting her off before she could finish her sentence. "And don't worry about them."

"How can we not?" Jillian asked. She pulled out her phone. "I've got a few calls to make. I'm certain we can pull together to give those kids a good Christmas."

"Absolutely," Hannah agreed. "Their Christmas makes mine sound like a tropical getaway."

I laid my hand over Jillian's, effectively blocking her phone from sight.

"I said, you don't need to worry about them."

"Zachary, if we don't do something then…" Jillian paused as she looked at me, her eyes widening. "You did something. What did you do?"

"Let's just say that they have a secret Santa keeping an eye on them."

"What did you do?" Jillian repeated. "Maybe I can help."

"I want to help, too," Hannah added.

"I'm telling you, I'm really starting to love small towns," I said, as I smiled at each of them. "You'll never find anyone in my old neighborhood doing this. I've got this covered, trust me. I've already spoken with Woody at Toy Closet. He's going to pick out an assortment of toys for both the kids and even add in a few things for the parents. I allotted $200, but didn't know if that was enough. I made Woody promise me he'd let me know if he went over. I'm also pretty sure that if he does then he still won't tell me. Anyway, to finish the job, he's going to have Zoe wrap them up."

Both women stared at me in utter silence.

"Now, that covers the presents," I continued, before either of them could say anything. "I also placed a call to Taylor, at Farmhouse Bakery. She's going to organize a delivery of some cookies and cupcakes later today, with whatever else she sees fit to add to the order. I figured … what? What is it?"

Both women were openly crying.

"What's wrong? I thought you guys would be happy. It's the least I could do."

Jillian rose from the couch and approached me. Uncertain of what was happening, I started to inch away. She pulled me into a hug and sobbed into my shoulder.

"That has got to be the most generous act of kindness I have ever witnessed. You don't know those people, do you?"

I shook my head. "No. What does that have to do with it?"

Hannah suddenly wrapped her arms around the two of us and it became a three-way hug. I waited in an awkward silence for a few moments while Jillian and Hannah composed themselves and finally broke the hug.

"That's so sweet, Zachary," Hannah told me. "Why did you do it?"

I shrugged. "Because it was the right thing to do, I guess. Christmas is, er, was my favorite time of year. I'd like to go back to enjoying the holidays again and the last thing I want to see is someone suffer during this time of year. I don't know who is responsible for these burglaries, but I sure will do everything I can to help Vance find him."

"Did Sherlock find anything at the second burglary?" Jillian asked.

I shook my head. "No. He kept fixating on the tree. He ignored the whole house and instead kept pulling me back to the decorated Christmas tree."

"Maybe he's telling us we need to check out the trees," Jillian suggested.

"I thought about that, too," I said. "Vance and I wanted to know if Sherlock was fascinated with all indoor trees so we ran an experiment."

"What kind of experiment?" Hannah wanted to know.

"We went outside where a crowd of onlookers had gathered and asked if anyone would let us into their house so we could check out their tree."

"Did anyone volunteer?" Jillian asked.

I shuddered. "Yes. Clara Hanson just happened to live next door."

Both Jillian and Hannah clapped their hands over their mouths. I shuddered again. Both women started giggling.

"It's not funny," I scolded. "That lady creeps me out."

"So, what did Sherlock think of her tree?" Jillian asked. "Was he just as fascinated by it?"

"Yep. The experiment was a bust. Sherlock only had eyes for the tree. That's what made me get the tree over there today. I wanted to see if Sherlock would be just as fascinated with my own as he was with those others."

"And was he?" Hannah asked.

I shook my head. "No. I can't figure him out. He acted like he couldn't care less. I thought maybe it was because it wasn't decorated. Now, thanks to you two, the house is covered in decorations and the tree looks fantastic. However, I've also watched Sherlock run by that tree several times. He hasn't even bothered to sniff it. So I'm thinking it was just a weird coincidence."

"I wonder how the thief got inside those houses," Hannah mused aloud.

"The first victim lived in an apartment," I reminded her. "The second was a house."

"And there were no signs of forced entry?" Jillian asked, frowning. "There must be something we're overlooking."

"Like what?" I asked. "No forced entry, no unlocked doors, and no open windows. How else would someone get inside?"

"If the police are going to figure out who is behind these thefts, then that's where they need to start," Jillian decided. "Identify which method the thief is using to get inside and they'll be one step closer to catching him. Or her. You never know nowadays."

"How could they make it inside?" Hannah asked.

The horizontal tornado passed by again, going at least Mach 3 without showing any signs of slowing down.

"You'd think they'd run out of energy," I mused.

"Colin can go for hours," Hannah said, giving me a smile. "That's why that boy puts away so much food, I'm sure."

"He had a healthy appetite, that's for sure," I added, eyeing the one lonely piece of pizza still sitting in the open box. "Anyway, I suggested to Vance that it was almost as if Santa Claus was taking back all the presents, since neither of us could figure out how the perp got inside."

"I'll wager they used a transporter," Jillian giggled.

"Dork," Hannah snorted, letting out a small giggle. "Could they have had a key?"

"How?" I asked. "We've already verified there weren't any keys hidden around the property."

"What if the thief found something unlocked and made sure to lock it once they left?" Jillian asked.

I shook my head. "I heard Vance ask that question at each crime scene. Each time the occupant swore inside and out that there was nothing left open or unlocked."

"What else is there?" Hannah asked.

"Chimney!" Colin blurted out as he sprinted by. Both corgis were still in pursuit.

"Good idea, kid," I called out as Colin disappeared from view. "Only I'm pretty sure Santa didn't do it," I muttered once he was out of earshot.

"I'd say that leaves only one option," Jillian announced. "Someone picked the lock."

"Vance said that the locks didn't look like they had been tampered with," I reminded her.

Colin and the dogs came back into the room. The boy was out of breath and still laughing as he claimed one of the recliners in the room. Sherlock and Watson padded up to him, saw that their prey was now motionless, and slid into down positions. After a moment or two they keeled over, as if their wind-up keys had finally wound down.

"I know two someones who will be sleeping well tonight," I observed.

Hannah looked at her son and smiled.

"Better make that three."

"Back to lock picking," I said. "I've always assumed that picking a lock would leave telltale signs on the lock itself that would prove it had been tampered with."

"Maybe for an amateur," Jillian said, "but what about a pro? If you knew what you were doing, could you pick a lock and not leave any marks or scratches on the locks?"

"Look it up."

We all looked over at the boy and saw that he had pulled a cell phone out of his pocket and was tapping and sliding his finger across the screen. He waited a few moments, tapped another set of commands, and then smiled. He held the phone up for us to see.

"See? It's possible."

"What did you do?" Hannah asked her son.

"I just Googled the answer, Mom," Colin said. "You always tell me to 'look it up' whenever I have a question and want to know the answer. Well, that's what Google is for. If you don't know, you ask it and it'll tell you."

"Google is not a person," Hannah corrected. "You

can't speak about an inanimate object like it has feelings."

"It says right here that it is possible to pick a lock without leaving any traces, provided you're an expert in lock picking. It takes a lot of expertise."

Colin handed me his phone as I made my way over to him. I looked at the article he was looking at. He had pulled up one of those Wiki websites.

"It also says that it takes time to do it without any noticeable marks. Thanks, Colin. That's incredibly helpful."

The boy beamed at this.

"Could the police take apart the locks and see if there are any scratches inside?" Hannah suggested. "Would they be able to tell if the lock was picked?"

I shrugged. "I guess it's possible. I do think that it's definitely worth passing along."

My phone rang just as I pulled it out of my pocket. I looked at the display and grunted. Well, well. Speak of the devil.

"Vance. Hey, I've got something you might be interested in. Is it possible to take apart the locks on those two burglaries and see if the lock could have been picked?"

"Maybe. Forget about that for now. Do you know where Birch Street is?"

I thought for a moment.

"South of Main?"

"Right. Get down here on the double."

I felt a chill go down my spine. Something was wrong. Vance was spooked and I didn't want to know what it would take to spook a police detective.

"What's the matter? What's happened?"

"There's been another burglary. And this time we have a body."

SIX

Do we know who it is?" I asked as soon as I arrived on scene and managed to get Vance's attention.

The dogs and I had been standing outside the scene of the third burglary for about twenty minutes now. Vance had informed me since the house was now the scene of a homicide, we wouldn't be allowed inside until the crime scene techs had done their preliminary investigation. I was pretty certain that Sherlock wouldn't be able to find anything once the CSTs had finished their work, but I also knew it couldn't hurt to try.

"The DB was a relative of the homeowner," Vance informed me, pulling out a familiar notepad. He flipped a few pages. "Mr. Jeremy Rutton, Portland. He's a nephew to Mr. Horace Rutton, owner of the house."

"DB?" I repeated, frowning.

"Dead body. Jeez, Zack. I thought you were a writer."

"I'm not a crime writer, thank you very much," I snapped in reply.

"What kind of books did you say you write again?" Vance asked, turning to look back at the house as police continued to swarm around it.

Swell. How was I going to get out of this one?

"Detective Samuelson!" a voice called out.

I breathed a sigh of relief. I had been saved by some woman who had just exited the house.

"Yes?" Vance said.

"As per your request, I contacted the locksmith. He said he'll be here in about fifteen minutes."

Vance nodded his thanks.

"We're leaving no stone unturned this time," Vance told me. "I want to know if the lock has been picked, so we have PV's new locksmith stopping by."

"As long as he doesn't give copies of the keys he makes to…"

"He doesn't and he won't," Vance assured me. "Apparently he's a retired policeman who's just looking for something to do. And to top it off, he's a friend of the captain, so if anything happens it'll be the captain who looks bad."

"It's good enough for me," I decided.

The last locksmith to call PV home had been caught with his hand in the proverbial cookie jar. Apparently, he had been making copies of all the keys that had come through his store and had been helping himself to their valuables whenever the homeowner went out of town. Call me paranoid, but I had every single lock changed yet again after that news broke, even paying through the nose to get a locksmith from Medford out to my house.

"So the vic is from out of town," I said. "That really stinks. So what do you think happened? Do you think the vic surprised the burglar by coming home early or do you think maybe the burglar thought the house was empty and made the mistake of breaking in?"

"Neither, although you're closer with option two."

"So the victim was home and the burglar surprised him," I deduced. "This marks the first burglary of an occupied house, doesn't it?"

"You didn't hear me," Vance pointed out. "You're close but not quite right. The burglar hit this house and stole all the presents, only there wasn't one person home, but two."

"What? Does that mean we have a witness who can identify the murderer?"

Vance shook his head. "No. The vic's girlfriend was in one of the guestrooms, taking a nap. She slept right through the break-in and the murder."

I whistled in amazement, "And I thought I was a heavy sleeper."

"She insists she's a very light sleeper," Vance argued, "and that she was only in the room for about fifteen minutes. Do you get that, Zack? This guy, whoever he is, managed to gain access to the house, steal the presents, and shoot the victim with what the ME thinks is a 9mm pistol. All without waking up the girl and he did this in only a few minutes."

"*How* did he do that?" I demanded.

"That's why you're here," Vance told me. "Third time's the charm. I'm hoping Sherlock finds something or else he's gonna lose his rep as Wonderdog."

A man appeared in the open doorway of the house and waved Vance and me over.

"There's our signal," Vance said, heading toward the house. "Apparently they think they've learned everything they need to and will allow you and the dogs in. Same rules as before. Don't touch anything. If Sherlock spots something then let me know, okay?"

"You got it. Sherlock, Watson, are you ready? Let's go see if we can find anything."

Both corgis, who had been sitting complacently on the sidewalk on either side of me, rose to their feet, shook themselves off—almost in perfect unison—and trotted alongside me as I headed toward the front door. We crossed into the house and I paused as I gave all the extra slack in the leash to the dogs. Sherlock glanced once up at me and immediately moved off. Watson followed closely behind.

One of the crime scene techs walked past us just then. The guy nodded his head when he saw me. The jingle of a collar caused him to look down and smile at the dogs.

"Which one is Sherlock?" the tech asked.

I pointed him out. "He's the one with the black fur."

"I hope he finds something," the tech confidentially told me.

"Why?" I asked, dropping my voice to a whisper. "Couldn't find anything in here?"

The tech shook his head. "Not a thing. Look around. This place should've been a smorgasbord for a thief, yet they only took what was under the tree."

"Just like before," I softly mused.

"Except for the DB. The perp must've thought this place was empty."

The tech moved off as I followed Sherlock around

the single-story home. We checked out bedrooms, several bathrooms, and the laundry room. Then we did a walk-through of the kitchen and garage. I eyed the living room and the large Christmas tree it contained and sighed. Lying dead center in the … Hmm. Poor choice of words. Directly in the middle of the room was the DB. There was also, thankfully, a circle of people around the body that hid it from sight. Good. The only problem was, the dogs and I still needed to check out the living room. Might as well get it over with.

"Come on, buddy," I said, giving Sherlock's leash a light tug. "Let's go see if there's anything worthwhile in the living room, okay? Ignore the thing in the middle of the room and try not to fixate on the tree, okay? I know you like Christmas trees."

And don't like mine, I mentally added. The little booger. Whatever.

Sure enough, as soon as we neared the tree Sherlock slowed and gazed up at it. He probably stared at it for a good ten seconds or so before turning to look at me as though I was a dummy for missing the obvious. I couldn't hide my groan.

"It's just a tree, pal. Nothing more. Let it go, okay?"

Surprisingly, Sherlock turned and then stared at a large potted plant sitting just inside the living room closest to the foyer. He pulled on his leash. If he wanted to look at a plant, fine. We'd look at the plant.

Sherlock nosed the pot a few times and then turned to look up at me. Well, color me intrigued. Remembering that we weren't supposed to touch anything I looked for Vance and saw him standing a dozen feet away, talking on his cell. I waved at him to get his attention.

Vance looked at me and mouthed, what? I pointed at the plant. Vance hurriedly terminated the call and rushed over.

"What did you find?"

"Not a clue. Sherlock stopped here and nudged the pot. Thought you ought to know. I wasn't about to go fishing around inside there to see what might be there."

Vance pulled out a pair of latex gloves and snapped them on. He squatted down next to the plant and gently pushed aside the foliage. He uttered a grunt of surprise. He reached inside and pulled out a shell casing.

"Well, well, well. What have we here?" Vance held the casing up to his nose and sniffed a few times. "Gunpowder. This shell has been fired recently. Zack, I do believe we have the shell casing from the gun that killed our vic." Vance turned to look at Sherlock, who was returning the stare. "Good job, boy. That's a *good* job. Our boys missed this."

We heard a knock at the door. Since we were already standing near the foyer, all we had to do was look up. A clean-cut older man wearing a pressed green business shirt and khakis, holding a large toolbox, was standing in the doorway.

"Excuse me, fellas. Did someone call for a locksmith?"

Vance nodded. He straightened, pulled out an evidence baggie from within his jacket pocket, and sealed the shell casing inside. He pulled off his glove and shook the man's hand.

"Detective Vance Samuelson."

"Jim Bennett. How can I help you, Detective?"

Vance pointed at the open front door.

"I need you to take that lock apart and tell me if it's

been picked. We're trying to figure out how this jackass got into the house unnoticed."

Jim nodded. "Happy to help. I'll get to work."

"So what kind of gun is that from?" I asked, as we stepped away from the locksmith and back into the living room. "Can you tell?"

"It came from a 9mm pistol," Vance said as he pulled the plastic baggie from his pocket. He held it up for me to see. "I don't think we'll be lucky enough to find a print, or even a partial print on this thing, but it's at least the first bit of evidence we have on this guy. I'll sic the lab boys on this just as soon as I get back to the station."

"This guy has gotta be stopped," I muttered as I looked around the house. "This is the third house he's hit in the last week. How long do you think it'll take before this town starts freaking out?"

Vance shook his head. "Not long at all. People are already calling in to report what they think is suspicious activity. The captain is gonna have to do something to address all these rumors. We've had people volunteering to go on patrol—armed, of course—to which we have to tell them that we have this under control. Do you want to know what the problem is?"

"You don't have it under control," I guessed.

Vance nodded. "Right. We don't. Hey, out of curiosity, did Sherlock show any interest in the tree?"

"Yep. He went straight to it, like a moth to flame. I wish I knew what he was looking at."

A smirk formed on my friend's face.

"Zack? He's looking at a tree. That's all."

"Possibly, but I can't help feeling like we're missing something."

Vance shrugged. "Perhaps. For now, I'll settle with knowing that the locks were picked."

"They weren't," Jim's voice said.

The locksmith motioned us over and showed us the disassembled lock he had pulled from the front door. He pulled a pen from his jacket pocket and began pointing at various pieces of the lock.

"If the lock had been picked then we'd see tiny scratches on the metal here, at the key hole, and in here, on the tumblers. There are several ways to pick a lock. Assuming that we're dealing with a pro, then they'd know this is a multi-tumbler lock. You'd insert a tension wrench in the bottom of the keyhole and then the pick is inserted at the top. To get the tumblers into position the pick is run back and forth, otherwise called 'scrubbing'. That sort of action would leave marks. I see no evidence of that here."

"So much for that theory," I grumbled.

"There is another option," Jim continued. "The lock could have been bumped."

"By what?" Vance asked.

"No, it could have been bumped open."

"The door can be bumped open?" I asked, appalled. "Talk about your shoddy workmanship. You'd think a front door would be more secure than that."

The locksmith shook his head. "No, not the door, but the lock."

"The lock can be bumped open?" Vance skeptically asked.

Jim nodded. "With the correct key, it can. You'd need a bumping key for that. Bumping keys can be made for each type of lock. Do you follow me?"

Both Vance and I shook our heads no.

"You take a key that'll fit the lock," Jim carefully explained. "You cut small grooves into the key, so that it looks like a miniature saw blade. The teeth in a bump key are set really low so that it can be fit into locks where the tumblers have been set low. The teeth are steep and jagged, so when you 'bump' the key while applying a little bit of torque, for a brief moment, the tumblers will bounce up into their unlock positions, thus allowing a window for you to open the lock. The torque you apply will make the tumblers stop once they reach the desired height."

Vance and I stared at each other in shock. Was this an actual viable method of obtaining entry into locked houses? How many people knew about this?

"Does a bumped lock leave any traces behind?" Vance wanted to know.

Jim shook his head. "No. If an amateur were to try bumping a lock, especially for the first time, then I'd say yes, but a bumping key, in the hands of an experienced professional, typically wouldn't leave a trace."

"How hard of a bump does it take to make the tumblers move?" I asked. "And what do they use to make the bump? A special tool?"

Once more Jim shook his head.

"There are special hammers that will do the job, but all it really takes is a firm tap on the key. All the demo videos I've seen show the tool used is the handle of a screwdriver."

"How many bumps does it take?" I asked.

"It depends on the lock," Jim answered. He had finished installing the dead bolt and was now working on the door knob. "It could be one bump or several. I will tell you that the most I've seen is four bumps."

"Which could be disguised as someone knocking on

the door," Vance surmised.

Jim nodded. "Right. In the hands of someone who knows how to use it, a thief could open any lock that he had a bumping key for, and disguise it as a simple knock on the door. When the person doesn't answer, then the thief will know there's no one home and in he goes."

"And what if there is someone home?" I asked.

Vance pointed at the potted plant. "Then we end up with a DB. That's why the casing was found in the plant. The thief knocked on the door to unlock it. If the girlfriend was asleep in the back bedroom then, I'd say the victim was also taking a nap, probably here on the couch. The guy is awakened by the knock, starts walking to the door, but is surprised by the thief who must've thought the house was vacant. The vic retreats into the living room and the perp shoots him from the entry."

"A DB?" Jim repeated, growing alarmed. "Someone died in here?"

Vance nodded. "The vic was a relative of the homeowner."

"I'm truly sorry to hear that," Jim said as he reassembled the lock and installed it back inside the door.

"So how does someone get one of these bumping keys?" I asked, still hung up on the simple fact that there was a 'master' key that could theoretically open any lock that it'd fit. "Have you made any before?"

Jim shook his head. "While familiar with the process, I could in theory make one, but I won't. It's all about having a strong code of ethics. I know full well that I could gain access to about ninety percent of all tumbler locks by simply carrying around nine or ten bumping keys, but I won't. It's the wrong thing to do."

"And if there's someone who doesn't have your same code of ethics?" Vance asked, frowning. "That would mean that they could get into any house they wanted."

"You may recall, but I've already had firsthand experience with one unscrupulous locksmith in recent months, remember?" I said.

"The process of bumping locks has been around for many years," Jim told us as he slid both door knobs into the door and tightened the mounting screws. Satisfied that everything was working properly, he began returning his tools to his toolbox.

I pulled out my own keys and held up the key that opens my house.

"Is this susceptible to being bumped?" I asked, certain I wouldn't like the answer.

Jim took my key and studied it.

"This will unlock a five tumbler lock. A bumping key would unquestionably open your door."

Vance pulled his own keys out and stared at his house key.

"I suppose mine is, too?"

Jim smiled at the both of us. "Ninety percent of tumbler locks, gentlemen. Yes, Detective, your house is susceptible, too."

"How do you stop something like this?" I demanded. "What about the ten percent that the bumping keys don't work on? Are there locks that are bump-proof?"

"If you're that worried, then I'd recommend a security system," Jim told us. He had finished packing his tools and was preparing to leave.

"You're telling me that there's no lock out there that is immune to this bumping technique?" Vance asked.

"If it's a basic tumbler lock, and if you see a keyhole, it

can be bumped," Jim told us. We had followed him outside and were now watching him load up his truck. "Look, fellas. There are locks that you can get that are bump proof. You've probably seen the locks with a digital keypad next to them?"

Both Vance and I nodded.

"If a lock doesn't need keys to open, then that means they're bump-proof. But, if you're that determined to keep a key-lock on your door, I do know of one from Master Lock that was specifically created to be bump-proof. I wish I could tell you how it works, but I haven't had a chance to install any yet. They're rather pricey."

"Consider me your first," I told the locksmith. "Sign me up. I'd like those locks on my house and my winery, please."

"You own a winery?" Jim asked, impressed. "Very nice. Which one?"

"Lentari Cellars."

"Get out of town. You own Lentari Cellars? My wife loves your Syrah!"

"Put a rush on this and I'll throw in a case of Syrah for your wife from our next harvest," I told the friendly locksmith.

Jim's eyes opened wide. He held out a hand.

"Deal."

"Sign me up, too," Vance told him.

Jim nodded. "You got it."

Just then, Vance's cell phone rang. He stepped aside to take the call. In the meantime, I pointed at Vance, and said to Jim, "The tab to change out his locks will be on me. It's going to be my Christmas present to him. He just doesn't know it yet."

Jim smiled. "You got it. It'll probably take me a few

days to get the locks shipped out. Can I swing by the winery to see how many locks I'm going to need?"

"Sure. You know what? Let's add one more house to that list. Are you familiar with the historic cottages here in town?"

Jim nodded. "A few. I haven't been in any, I'm sorry to say."

"One of them, Carnation Cottage, is off of Oregon Street. I'd like to change out the locks on that one, too."

"Who lives there?" Jim asked.

"Another friend. I'll tell her to expect you sometime in the next day or so if that's okay with you. You know what? Why don't you call me when you have everything ready?"

"What, are you this town's secret Santa or something?" Jim good-naturedly asked.

"It sure does feel like it lately," I told him. "That's okay. It's the right time of year for this type of thing. You'll let me know when you're ready?"

Jim nodded and held out a hand, "I will. You know, I never caught your name."

"Sorry. Zack Anderson."

Jim's eyebrows shot up.

"You're the guy who…"

"…was accused of murder," I finished for the locksmith after he had trailed off. "Yep, that's me. It was just one big misunderstanding."

We shook hands and I watched Jim stash his toolbox in the back of his truck. Then I heard a dog collar jingle. Sherlock and Watson had risen from where they had been lying and were ready to go. I had just loaded both dogs into my Jeep when Vance finished his call. He hurried over.

"Well, it's official, sports fans. Captain Nelson has

called for a meeting. It sounds like he's invited the whole town."

"I would imagine he wants to allay everyone's fears," I told my friend. "Are you against this?"

"Do you have any idea how this town will react once they find out that there's some guy running around with a key that can open their houses?"

Jim had just slid behind the wheel of his truck. He rolled the window down and leaned out. I noticed and nudged Vance on the shoulder.

"I don't know how you feel about full disclosure," Jim started, "but if I were you, I'd leave the part about bumping locks out of your report. At least until you can find the guy responsible for this."

Vance nodded. "In the meantime, I'd suggest you order as many of those bump-proof locks that you can get your hands on. Sooner or later this news will break and you're going to be inundated with requests for people to change out their locks."

Jim's friendly smile vanished.

"You have a point. I think I will. Good day to you both, gentlemen."

I felt a tug on a leash. Sherlock had wandered over to a section of the sidewalk that had a few tire marks on it, as though someone had tried to pull a U-turn in the middle of the road and had driven up on the curb. He sniffed the marks a few times and turned to look at me. As soon as he saw that I was looking, he turned back to the marks and woofed.

I wandered over and squatted down next to the corgi to drape an arm around him.

"What did you find, buddy? Some tire marks? Do you

think these belong to our suspect?"

Sherlock kept his nose glued to the ground. I looked up and down the sidewalk. There were tire marks everywhere. What were the chances that these were made by the perp's car?

"What's going on?" Vance asked, coming up behind me. "What are you looking at?"

"Tire marks."

"I can see that, Einstein. What about them?"

"Sherlock led me over here."

Vance glanced down at the tri-color corgi. He squatted down to give the marks a closer inspection. He looked both left and right.

"There are marks everywhere," Vance told me. "It's almost as if the people around here are lousy drivers. There are tire marks up and down the curbs."

"Yet he's only interested in these," I pointed out.

Vance pulled out his phone and snapped a few pictures.

"A valid point. All right, I'll see what I can find out about them."

"Were there any tire tracks around any of the other burglaries?" I asked.

Vance thought about it for a moment.

"None around the apartment complex. I mean, there were, but nothing we could use."

"And the doctor's house?" I asked.

Vance started sliding his finger along the phone's display. Then he tapped a message and then traced a few gestures on the screen. Then he tapped his phone a few times more and held it up to his ear.

"Jerry, this is Vance. Hey, you processed the scene from the burglary yesterday, right? Yes, the doctor's house.

Look, did you find any tire tracks outside? You did? Hmm. What's that? No, there's nothing wrong. It's just that there are some tire tracks out here. I'd like you to ... what? Sure. I'll hold."

"What's going on?" I asked in a hushed tone.

Vance tapped the phone's display, muting the call.

"He put me on hold. He had another call."

"This Jerry person isn't presently on scene?" I asked, confused.

"They're both processing the scene, only I saw Jerry leave a little bit ago to start logging the evidence," Vance explained. "The presence of a DB has the unfortunate side effect of canceling PTO. If we would have had more than ... Jerry? Yes. I'm still here. Right. I was asking about tire tracks. Did you find any yesterday? You did? I'd like you to compare them to a couple of pictures I just sent you. I've got reason to believe they might be involved. I ... sure, I'll hold again." Vance looked at me and gave me a thumbs up. "He got the pics and is checking them now."

At that moment ,my own cell phone began to ring.

"Zachary? It's Jillian. I'm sorry to bother you but I was just checking to make sure you're okay."

"Hi, Jillian. We're all good here," I assured her. "Hey, now that I have you on the phone, I've got something to run by you."

"Of course. What can I help you with?"

"The new locksmith was out here. Vance wanted to see if the locks had been tampered with so he had the locks taken apart."

"And were they?"

"Sadly, no. However..." I trailed off as I thought about

the best way to let her know that practically every house in PV was vulnerable to this thief. I took a deep breath. "However, the locksmith did point something out that could help a thief break in to your home. As a result, I'm having all the locks on the house and the winery switched over."

"Oh, no! Is it that bad?"

"Vance put in an order, too."

"Do you think I should get my locks replaced, too?"

I smiled. That was exactly what I was hoping to hear.

"I already ordered them for your house, too. My treat. Consider it an early Christmas present."

"Zachary Anderson, you don't have to buy new locks for my house. I'm perfectly capable of buying my own."

"I figured you could," I told her. "However, this is something I'd like to do for you. Now, smile and thank me for looking out for your well-being."

A few seconds of silence passed. I fidgeted nervously. Had I crossed the line by taking Jillian's safety into my own hands?

"Thank you, Zachary. That means a lot."

I let out the breath I had been holding.

"You're welcome."

"May I make a request?"

"Sure. What can I do for you?"

"Would you please have that locksmith take care of Hannah's house, too? And Taylor's. I'll pay for it, of course."

"I'll be sure to let the locksmith know."

Both Vance and I ended our calls at the same time. Vance looked at me with a victorious expression on his face. Curious, I cocked my head at him.

"What is it?"

Vance clapped my back.

"Jerry confirmed the tracks are a match to those he found at the doctor's place. We have our first viable lead!"

SEVEN

"Why are there four forks on the table?" I asked the following day.

The following Saturday, Vance, Harry, and I had decided to meet for lunch at a new—for me—restaurant. At my suggestion. I wanted to be able to show Jillian that I was at least trying to step out of my comfort zone. A little bird had told me that this was one of Jillian's favorite places to eat, so I thought I'd give them a try. While I knew almost immediately that there wasn't going to be anything on the menu that I'd like, I did want to give it a trial run first to see if I'd be able to bring Jillian here and find something that I'd be willing to try. I eyed the menu in front of me and sighed inwardly. This wasn't gonna be easy.

We were sitting at Chateau Restaurant & Wine Bar, less

than two blocks from Jillian's store. This place was far and away the nicest, ritziest restaurant here in town. Waiters were decked out in tuxedos; menus were printed on thick parchment and adhered to thin wooden backing. And … there were way too many pieces of silverware on the table to know what to do with.

I had eyed my friends when I first sat down. Harry, surprisingly enough, seemed to be at ease as he placed his thick cloth napkin on his lap. A check on Vance confirmed he looked as out of place as I must have.

"They probably provide spares in case you drop one," Vance guessed.

Harry shook his head. He leaned forward and tapped each of the pieces of silverware in front of him. He started with the fork on the far left.

"This is the fish fork," Harry began. "It's provided in case you order a fish dish."

I had to stifle a laugh. A fish fork? Seriously?

"And if we don't?" Vance asked under his breath. "I don't like fish."

"Then, after you place your order, they'll take it away," Harry casually explained. He caught sight of the approaching waiter. "Who's up for a bottle of wine? My treat, guys."

Vance looked at his watch and shrugged. "It's late enough. Why not? Zack, what do you say?"

"I say I'd rather have a Coke Zero," I muttered as the waiter arrived at our table to take our drink orders.

Harry grinned and nudged Vance, "That's more for us, right pal?"

Vance nodded and gave Harry a fist bump.

"Would you like to order a bottle of wine?" the waiter

eagerly asked, having overheard part of our conversation.

Harry nodded. "You bet. What would you recommend, man?"

The waiter thought for a moment.

"We were finally able to restock our supply of a local favorite, namely the Syrah produced by none other than Lentari Cellars. It is top rated and presently in high demand. It's only $149 per bottle. Shall I open one for you?"

I had been taking a sip from my water glass when I nearly choked.

"$149?" I sputtered, wiping the flecks of water from my mouth with my napkin. "You're selling a bottle of wine from Lentari Cellars for $149? Wow. I'm going to need to talk to Caden about our prices. That's too high."

The waiter gave me an appraising stare.

"You want to lower the prices? Of the wine obtained from Lentari Cellars? How could you possibly do that? We can barely get them on the phone to replenish our stock."

"What's your name?" Harry jovially asked the waiter.

"Ferdinand."

"Ferdinand, meet Zack Anderson, owner of Lentari Cellars."

Ferdinand's eyes shot open. He looked at me and then at Vance, as if waiting for him to confirm or rebuke what Harry had just said. Vance shrugged and picked up his own glass of water.

"Please wait here," Ferdinand instructed before rushing off.

"Where exactly are we going to go?" Harry called after him. He looked back at the two of us and shrugged. "Okay, picking up from where we left off. As I was saying, this is the fish fork. Then we have the dinner fork and salad fork."

I stared at the multitude of flatware on either side of my plate. I pointed at the lone fork on the right of the plate, lying to the right of two knives and a spoon. I squinted at it. It was much smaller than the others.

"What about this one?" I asked, tapping the tiny fork.

"That's probably the shellfish fork," Harry said as he picked his own up. "See the tines? There's only two. It's used to crack into the shells of oysters and such."

"He really knows his fork etiquette," Vance chuckled.

"He didn't use to," I said, giving Harry a bemused expression. "Where'd you learn about this?"

"From Julie," Harry answered. "Any time I acted out, or got on her bad side, she would make me dress up and take her out to the fanciest restaurant she could find. Trust me, I know all about this stuff. Way more than I'd like, if you catch my drift."

Ferdinand returned just then, followed closely by a second man, also wearing a tuxedo. He was older, in his mid-fifties, and was carrying a thick binder with various tabs sticking out at all angles. When Ferdinand continued to stand in silence, observing, the older man nudged him on the shoulder.

"Oh, I'm sorry. This is Mr. Enzo Dubois. He is the owner. Mr. Dubois, may I present Mr. Zachary Anderson, owner of Lentari Cellars."

I turned to look at the newcomer. Mr. Dubois was tall, lean, balding, and sported a pencil moustache. While unsure of what the proper response was, I figured I should at least offer a greeting from a standing position.

I rose to my feet, prompting Harry and Vance to join me. I extended a hand and waited to see what Mr. Dubois would do. After a second of two of hesitation, the restaurant owner clasped my hand with his own.

"Mr. Anderson! You are known to us, good sir!"

Mr. Dubois spoke with a heavy French accent.

"Good afternoon," I carefully returned. "It's a pleasure. Allow me to introduce my friends. This is Detective Vance Samuelson, of the PVPD, and this is Doctor Harrison Watt, town vet."

Mr. Dubois shook hands with everyone.

"A pleasure to meet you all! Especially you, Monsieur. You are the owner of Lentari Cellars, oui?"

I nodded. "Yes. Is there something I can do for you?"

"We are almost sold out of every bottle of wine you have provided us. We have but one case remaining of the Syrah and two of the gewürztraminer. Your wine is the talk of the town, monsieur! I am embarrassed to admit this, but I am unable to raise anyone at the winery. I need to order more! We cannot run out now. Please, monsieur. Will you help me?"

"I'm pretty sure my winemaster handles all the ordering," I told the friendly owner. "I know the wine has become very popular once we restarted production, only I had no idea it was this popular. It's all supply and demand. Right now it seems we cannot keep up with the demand. Perhaps if we…" I hesitated when I saw the owner's face fall. "Look. I can't make any guarantees, only that I'll check with Caden. We might have a case or two stashed away in a back room."

Mr. Dubois caught my hand and pumped it vigorously.

"I can't thank you enough, Mr. Anderson! We will take whatever you can provide us. I don't know how to thank you. *Mais oui!* I know what I can do for you. Your lunch today is on me! I insist!"

About ready to object, I remembered the $149 price

tag on the bottle of wine Harry and Vance wanted. I gave the owner a friendly smile. I nodded.

"You've got yourself a deal, Mr. Dubois."

The owner and waiter hurried away, chatting excitedly with one another. Harry grinned at me and held up an open hand. I gave him a high-five.

"Bro, you just saved me at least $300 bucks."

"And I'll find some way to collect," I assured him, giving Vance a conspiratorial wink.

We placed our orders a few minutes later. Harry ordered some type of steak that I couldn't pronounce while Vance ordered lobster. When it came to my turn, I figured I'd be safe with seafood Alfredo.

Words cannot even begin to describe how wrong I was. I not only managed to gross myself out but Vance, too. More on that later. Once we had our food, Vance decided to fill us in with what he knew about the case.

"I assume you want to know about the tire tracks," Vance began, as he pulled his notebook from his back pocket.

"Yeah, bro," Harry said between mouthfuls of steak and mushrooms. "You're the one who wanted to meet for lunch. Let's hear it!"

"The tracks on the curb that I took pictures of match those taken by one of our techs, Jerry, outside the retired dentist's house."

"Is that burglary number one or two?" Harry asked. He took a sip of wine and sighed contentedly. "Man, I love this stuff. You make a great wine, Zack."

"Thank Caden, not me," I corrected. "Sorry, Vance. Go ahead."

"Right. As I was saying, the marks are a match. They've

identified the tire as a LT245 75R16. This particular model is manufactured by BFGoodrich."

I picked around a yellowish-orange something-or-other on my plate and ate another forkful of pasta.

"You can tell that by looking at the tread pattern?" I asked, amazed.

"There's an online database of nothing but tire treads and shoe tracks," Vance informed us. "It helps to know what we're dealing with."

"So what kind of car uses those tires?" Harry wanted to know. "Is it very specific or is it a very generic model of tire that is found on every Tom, Dick, and Harry's car?"

"We're waiting on the full report. I'm told we'll have it within the hour. Once we get it, we should be able to see what cars it typically comes installed on."

Right about this time I finished eating all the 'edible' parts of my lunch. The only part left was the 'seafood' part of Seafood Alfredo. Assuming this meant there was perhaps little bits of cut up fish, I chose a piece of seafood that was a light yellow in color and about the size of standard meatball. Not wanting the blasted thing to go jetting off the plate if I cut into it incorrectly, I grabbed one of the knives and sliced it in half.

Green ooze poured out.

My stomach roiled at the sight. I closed my eyes and pushed the plate away, breathing heavily. I also noticed that all activity at our table had ceased. I opened my eyes and looked over at Vance. He was leaning forward and peering at the growing puddle of green goo on my plate with a look of utter disgust on his face.

"Dude, what *is* that? You didn't eat that, did you?"

Harry leaned forward and studied the spectacle with

a quizzical look on his face. He reached out with his fork, speared half of the thing, and brought it over to his plate. After a few moments of careful inspection, he shrugged and popped it in his mouth.

I nearly came out of my seat. He might as well have eaten a live cockroach. Thankfully, I wasn't the only one.

"That has got to be the nastiest thing I have ever witnessed," Vance murmured, keeping his voice low. "And you're talking to a homicide detective, pal. Remember that."

"I'm not sure what it is," Harry thoughtfully said as he chewed. "There's a briny taste, so maybe it's an oyster? I just haven't seen one that big before."

I couldn't even look at my plate. Whatever it was, I could smell it. My stomach started to churn again. I chugged down my soda, and then polished off my water. Vance wordlessly slid his water over to me. I drained his glass, too.

"Well, I'm done. Shall we?"

An hour later, we were sitting in Vance's living room around a card table. The poker chips were out and we were several rounds into a game of Texas Hold 'Em poker. The front door opened and the women walked in. Tori, Julie, and Jillian came in carrying bags of groceries.

"Need any help?" I automatically asked as I looked up.

Jillian beamed a smile at me, "No, thank you. We've got it. Thank you for asking."

"Kiss-ass," Vance muttered. "That kind of stuff makes the rest of us look bad."

"It's a force of habit," I admitted. "I did that for Samantha all the time."

"I think it's a sweet move," Harry said as he dealt another round of cards. "I do that for Julie, too."

"You're both brown-nosers," Vance grumbled. "Come on, come on. Deal the river. Let's see what we're working with here."

The women pulled up chairs and joined us as the game continued.

"So can anyone look at that database?" I asked as the three of us tossed our ante into the pot.

Vance looked up. "Huh?"

"That tire tread database. You said that the police have some way to input in the treads from a tire and it'll tell you what the tire is. Can anyone look at it?"

"You need permission," Vance said. He glanced at his cards, studied the flop, and folded. "Why?"

"I just think it's remarkable that you can input a picture and a computer can tell you what tire made it."

"It's not much different than scanning a fingerprint and letting the computer look for a match," Vance said. "Think of it like a fingerprint for a vehicle."

Right on cue Vance's phone beeped, signaling an incoming text message. The detective pulled his phone out of his pocket. After a few moments, he put the phone on the table and grinned at me.

"Ask and ye shall receive."

"Was that the report you were waiting for on the tire tracks?" Julie asked.

Vance nodded. "Yep. Listen up. The LT245 75R16 is an all-terrain tire."

"How does that help us?" I asked.

"That tire isn't found on passenger cars," Vance answered. "It's used on full-sized pickups."

"So you're looking for a truck," Harry quipped as he dealt another round. "That would make sense. You need cargo room to be able to haul around the loot they've been making off with."

"Have you found any tire tracks around the apartment complex?" Jillian asked.

Vance sighed. "Yes, and that's the problem. It's an apartment complex. There were tons of tracks. There were so many that it pretty much killed any chance of looking for individual tracks."

Jillian's face fell. "Oh. Sorry."

"It's not your fault," Vance kindly told her.

"I have an idea," Tori announced.

Five pairs of eyes settled on the tall redhead.

"Why don't you go over everything you know from each case?" Tori suggested. "It'll help refresh your memory as well as bring everyone else up to speed. What do you think?"

Vance shrugged. He looked down at his notebook and started flipping pages. Growing exasperated when, after a few pages he still hadn't hit the beginning of PV's latest crime spree, he wet the tip of his finger with his tongue and flipped faster.

"Here we are. Okay. We'll start with the first burglary. This would've been last week, on Friday. The Murphy family was hit at the apartment complex on the west side of town."

"That small one not far from the library?" Jillian asked.

Vance nodded. "Right. A family of four lives there. Husband, wife, and two small kids. The kids were in school and both parents were working. We know that the apartment was hit during business hours, which means the perp did this in broad daylight. We also know they ignored everything else in the apartment and just focused on the presents under the tree. Now, at the time, we figured it was because the apartment lacked any items of value."

"Don't forget the part about no signs of forced entry," I reminded Vance.

"Right. There were no broken windows, or busted down doors. There wasn't even any sign of trauma on the locks. Whoever was making it inside was doing so as though he had a key to the place."

"Well, could he?" Julie asked.

Vance shook his head. "No. We already verified there were no hidden keys outside the apartment and those who had the extra keys, namely the apartment manager and his assistant, had them under lock and key. So, how the thief gained entry inside remains a mystery."

"Did you know someone donated a bundle of toys to the family?" Julie suddenly asked. "It was all the girls at the station could talk about today. I just wish we would have thought of it first."

I'm sure my face flamed up, but I didn't say anything. I managed to look away before Jillian could catch me grinning. She was the only one in the group who knew I was behind the donated bundle of toys. She took my hand in hers and pretended she didn't know anything about it.

"Dr. Bowen—the station's psychologist—said the mother was eternally grateful," Julie continued. "She said that their Christmas was now going to be better than they originally thought."

"Someone donated some food, too," Vance added, looking up from his notebook. "Someone donated cookies, cupcakes, bagels, and one of those round cakes with a hole in the middle."

"A Bundt cake?" Tori guessed.

Jillian's hand tightened in my own. Taylor had been included in on the secret, seeing how her store was responsible for the donation of the baked goodies. Woody, too, for that matter, since he was the one supplying the presents. Jillian laced her fingers through mine and held on tight.

"Okay, moving on," Vance announced. He flipped a page in his notebook. "Monday's robbery. It happened at the home of a retired dentist, Dr. David Morris."

"His house was a lot nicer," I recalled.

"He had the bucks, no doubt about it," Vance agreed. "This was where we realized that money was not a motivating factor for these burglaries. That house was dripping with money. Top notch home theater system. Jewelry box. Floor safe. Original pieces of art. Nothing was touched. Nothing that is, except for the presents under the tree. Our Grinch stole every single one of them."

"Again, without any signs of forced entry," I added.

"That's right," Vance agreed. "No hidden keys. No unlocked doors or open windows. And I should also point out that the window of opportunity here was probably no more than an hour or so."

"How did you come to that conclusion?" Harry asked.

"The doctor said he and his wife had stepped out for lunch," Vance answered. "Those were the only plans they had for the day."

"They must have been watched," Tori guessed. "It's the only thing that makes sense."

"If that's the case, then how did the thief know they'd even leave at all?" Vance asked as he looked over at his wife. "How would this Grinch character have known what they were planning on doing? It doesn't make any sense."

"What about the presents?" Julie asked. "Could there have been something that was wrapped up that this … I'm sorry, what are you calling him?"

"The Grinch," Vance, Harry, and I all repeated, in unison.

"Okay, the Grinch. Do you think the Grinch might have been looking for something in particular?"

Jillian frowned. "Maybe, but do you really think that whatever the Grinch was looking for could have been found under the Murphy's tree? I can see where it might have been under Dr. Morris' tree, but not at the first burglary."

Julie sat back in her chair and nodded. "True. I hadn't thought of that."

"Now, for the third burglary," Vance said, flipping a few more pages. "This happened the following day, on Tuesday. It was at the home of another affluent citizen. Once more, there were no signs of forced entry and, as before, all the presents were stolen."

"Only this time somebody was killed," Jillian quietly added.

Vance nodded. "Sad, but true. Now, the vic is the nephew of the home owner. He was visiting from out of town and, we think, asleep on the couch when the burglar broke in."

"He broke in?" Harry repeated. "They finally found out how they were getting in?"

Vance shook his head. "No. Sorry. Poor choice of words. What I meant to say was, when the burglar illegally entered the house, the vic was asleep on the couch. The burglar fired a single shot, which struck the man in his chest. He, unfortunately, died on the scene."

"Do we know when this was?" Tori asked. "I assume the neighbors heard the gunshot?"

"No," Vance groaned. "We figure he must have had a silencer on the gun. No one heard anything. In fact, the guy's girlfriend was asleep and slept through the entire burglary as well as the murder. She said she didn't hear a thing."

"And still no signs of forced entry," I added, this time forcing a smile.

"Confirmed by a locksmith," Vance agreed. "He took the lock apart and verified that it hadn't been picked."

"So how is the Grinch getting inside?" Harry demanded. "No key, no open windows, no broken doors. This is freakin' crazy, man."

"I never said they didn't have a key," Vance contradicted, giving everyone a coy smile.

"Yes, you did," Tori countered. "I heard you specifically say that there weren't any keys hidden around the house. So where would they have gotten a key?"

Vance reached into a pocket and held up a shiny gold key.

"They would have brought their own."

I stared at the key. I noticed right away that the teeth of the key were all uniform, looking exactly like a saw blade. Somehow, and I don't know how, Vance had got his hands on one of those bumping keys.

"So they had keys to these houses?" Harry asked. He smiled. "Then that should be easy. Find out who has given someone their copies and you should have your man. By the way, didn't the previous locksmith end up going to jail for giving away copies of the keys he made?"

Vance nodded. "Yep. He's still sitting in a jail cell,

waiting to be tried in Medford."

I pointed at the key.

"Where'd you get that?"

"Jim made it for me," Vance said as he tossed the key to me, "but only after he made me promise I wouldn't hold him responsible."

"It's just a key," Julie pointed out. "What's the big deal?"

Vance took the key from my hand, stood, and walked to his front door.

"I'll show you why this is a big deal. This key will open any tumbler lock that it safely fits into."

Curious, the rest of us rose to our feet and followed Vance to the front door.

"You mean that's some type of master key?" Harry asked, confused. "How can that be? Locks are supposed to be secure, aren't they? One key should not open them all."

"This is called a 'bumping' key," Vance explained, as he opened the front closet. He pulled out a small tool box and selected a regular screwdriver. "Our new locksmith demonstrated this for me. It … well, see for yourself. Honey, could you hand me my key ring? It's on the end table there."

Tori passed her husband his keys. My detective friend selected his house key, held it up for everyone to see, and then held the bumping key up next to it. Everyone could see that the teeth were nowhere close to being the same. There shouldn't have been any way that the bumping key would unlock the door. Vance opened the door, and with the door still open, pointed at the deadbolt sitting several inches above the regular door lock.

"Watch this. I've locked the deadbolt here. Now, the normal house key unlocks it, like this." Vance inserted the key and twisted. The lock retracted into the door. He twisted the lever on the deadbolt from the other side of the door and relocked it. "Now, thanks to the pins and tumblers inside the lock, any key whose grooves don't match exactly right will then be denied access. Observe."

Vance inserted the bumping key and tried to unlock the deadbolt. Unsurprisingly, it refused to open. He pulled the key back out and made a show of holding it up so that we could see he hadn't swapped it out with his house key. Vance reinserted the bumping key into the lock. This time he held the key in two fingers, applied a little bit of pressure by twisting the key, and tapped the head of the key with the butt end of the screwdriver.

The deadbolt popped open.

"What the h—!" Harry swore, covering the distance to the door in just a few steps. He stooped down to stare at the deadbolt. "Do that again."

Vance repeated the trick. Once more the deadbolt popped open. Vance pulled the bumping key out and demonstrated it was just as effective in the main lock as it was in the deadbolt. Within seconds, he had opened both locks using the bumping key. All he had done was knock a few times on the top of the key as it was sticking out of the lock.

"I think I'm going to be sick," Tori gasped. "That means the Grinch could strut right in here and do whatever he wanted to do to us. Vance, you need to do something about this!"

Vance nodded. "I already have, my dear. Jim Bennett, that'd be the new locksmith, has already ordered new locks that are specifically designed to be bump-proof. He got nearly a dozen in earlier today. He's already agreed to stop by tomorrow—on a Sunday—and change out the locks. Speaking of which…" Vance turned to me and pointed an accusing finger. "Would you care to explain why I was told that there wouldn't be any charge to replace the locks?"

I grinned at Vance and Tori.

"It's a Christmas present, guys. That's all. Say thanks."

Tori rushed over to give me a hug. Tears were in her eyes. She held on to me for a few moments before she finally pulled away.

"You have no idea how much that means to me," she sniffed.

"You have two beautiful girls," I told her. "You don't screw around with a family's safety."

"That was awful sweet of you," Julie told me, giving me a hug as well.

"I was going to pay for yours, too," I told her, eliciting a gasp from her, "but Vance argued that he was paying it forward. So Vance took care of yours."

"What?" Julie gasped, turning to look at Vance.

"Dude!" Harry exclaimed. He and Julie pulled Vance into an awkward three-way hug. "You didn't have to do that!"

"Don't worry about it," Vance told them. "And you're next, after us. Then Jim has agreed to take care of Jillian's cottage next."

Jillian smiled warmly at me and gave me a hug.

"Thank you."

"You told her," Vance guessed.

"I had to. I couldn't have a stranger showing up at her door. It'd freak her out. So I had to let her in on it."

"Okay," Vance announced, clapping his hands and rubbing them together, as though they were cold, "we're making progress. We have method of entry. Now all we need is motivation. Why is the Grinch only stealing presents? Does anyone have any thoughts on the matter?"

"I still say they're looking for a very specific something," Julie said.

"That's one theory," Vance said. "Any other suggestions?"

"Maybe whoever is doing this hates Christmas?" Jillian suggested. "Hence the Grinch moniker?"

"Possible," Vance agreed.

"The Grinch has a thing for Christmas paper?" I suggested.

Vance's cell beeped once before he could respond. He grabbed it from the card table and read the message. He nodded and held up the phone, as if he was had found a gold nugget.

"I've got the report on the tire tracks, if anyone is interested."

"Oh yeah," I said. "Let's hear it."

"As I mentioned before, this specific brand of tire isn't found on passenger cars. Its all-terrain, which means it can handle off-road conditions. It comes standard on several full-sized pickup trucks and Econoline vans."

"What's an Econoline van?" I asked, confused.

"It's a cargo van," Vance answered. "Ford makes 'em."

I suddenly thought of Sherlock and the times that he had barked at the Square L.

"A cargo van? You mean like a kidnapper van?"

Vance laughed. "Yeah. That's one way to describe them."

"A kidnapper van?" Jillian repeated, with a puzzled expression on her face. "What do you mean by that?"

"Haven't you ever seen the movies or television shows where a person is abducted?" I asked. "The kidnappers always appear to be driving a windowless cargo van."

"And they're always white," Harry added with a knowing grin. "It would take one gutsy individual to drive one of those things around. Might as well paint the word 'predator' on the side of it."

"That doesn't really help us," Tori decided. "There's probably tons of those in town."

"In Pomme Valley?" Julie asked. "I haven't seen any."

"Except I have," I said excitedly. "Every time I see it Sherlock barks his fool head off at it."

Vance looked up, his eyes sharpening.

"Sherlock has barked at a white cargo van? Here in town? Zack, why didn't you tell me?"

"And tell you what?" I demanded. "Inform you that Sherlock has barked at a dozen different cars today? For all we know Tori is right. There are probably dozens of those vans in town."

Vance dialed a number into his cell.

"Detective Samuelson requesting a records check. Yes, Sandy, I know it's the weekend and you're covering the desk by yourself. I just need to know if there are any white cargo vans registered in PV. No, no specific model. Any will do. You will? Thanks. I look forward to your call."

Vance hung up and gave me a strange look.

"What?" I asked.

"How many times has Sherlock barked at this van?"

I shrugged. "A few. I don't remember. Why?"

"New rule. From now on, whenever we're working a case together, if Sherlock expresses interest in anything, no matter how insignificant, you are to let me know, okay?"

I laughed and shook my head. "I can see it now. 'Hey, buddy. Sherlock took a dump, turned around, and barked at it. Then a fluttering leaf caught his attention and he followed that for twenty yards before barking at it.' Are you sure you want me to do that?"

"If this pans out, yes I do."

"How long will it take to find out if there are any white cargo vans in PV?" Jillian asked.

"The database is pretty specific," Julie automatically answered. "Sandy is good. She should have the results in about…"

Vance's cell rang. I grinned at Julie.

"Wow, you're good."

"Detective Samuelson. Sandy, hello. What do you have? Really. That's what I need to know. Thank you. I appreciate it."

"Well?" I prompted. "What did you find out?"

"There are exactly zero registered white cargo vans that call PV home."

"Oh, come on," I protested. "PV isn't that small. There must be one or two somewhere around here."

Vance nodded. "There is. And I'd like to find that van to see if the tread matches."

He began punching numbers into his cell.

"Who are you calling now?" Tori asked.

"I'm calling the captain. I'm asking permission to send out an APB on that van. This is too good of an opportunity to pass up. I'll bet you any amount of money that van's tires will be a match."

"Are you sure you want to bet again?" Tori asked, stifling a giggle. "You lost the last one and I'm sure you will remember what's involved with that, right?"

Vance's face blushed bright red.

"Let's not get into that now, okay? We have more important things to talk about."

The bet in question dealt with a certain detective friend of mine having to wear tights and learn how to tap dance. He foolishly made a wager that Sherlock couldn't find the missing pendant from the mummy case a few months ago. Well, Sherlock found it. I cannot wait to see Vance outfitted in his Peter Pan costume.

"Says who?" Harry demanded. "This sounds juicy. Spill, dude. What about that bet? You lost? What did you lose?"

I quietly texted Harry's cell, promising to fill him in later.

EIGHT

Early Sunday afternoon the dogs and I were headed for the back storeroom of the winery. Since I had made a deal with Mr. Dubois, and essentially cost his restaurant hundreds of dollars in revenue for that miserable excuse of a lunch, I figured the least I could do was search my winery's storeroom and see if I could locate any extra bottles of wine. There had to be a case or two tucked away in a dark corner. Somewhere.

I unlocked Lentari Cellars and stepped inside the storefront, locking the doors after me only once I verified both Sherlock and Watson had followed me in. Both corgis turned to look up at me, no doubt wondering what I was doing in here on a Sunday afternoon when, instead, we typically watched a movie or played inside with any one of the hundreds of toys they left scattered all over my living room. I pointed at one of the display racks and tapped a bottle of Syrah.

"We're looking for some more of this, guys. Sherlock? You're good at finding things. Let's see how good you really are. The storeroom is back there, through those doors. If his Royal Highness would allow me to open the door for you…"

Sherlock snorted and looked away. So much for that. Apparently, since this wasn't part of any police investigation then he wasn't interested. Little snot. I was stooping down to unclip their leashes when I heard the distinct sound of a key being inserted into the lock outside. I peered around the racks and saw someone—wearing dark clothes—fiddling with the lock.

What do I do? Call for the police? Who else has a key to that door besides me?

"Zack? Where are you at? I know you're in here."

I visibly relaxed. It was Caden. What he was doing here, on a Sunday, was beyond me.

"I'm over here," I said, stepping out from behind the rack. "What are you doing here? Better yet, how'd you know I was here?"

Caden closed the door behind him and held up a satchel he had slung over a shoulder. It could have doubled for a laptop bag. He opened the bag and pulled out a wine bottle.

"What are you doing with that?" I suspiciously asked.

Caden grinned as he waved the bottle in front of me.

"I saw the dogs go in. Hi Sherlock. Watson. Zack, I'm glad you're here. I think I'm finally ready for you to try a sample of my latest and greatest experiment."

"Aww, crap. You're gonna make me taste that? I don't have any soda with me."

"You'll be fine," Caden assured me. He reached behind the small bar counter that was in the far corner of the showroom and pulled out two wine glasses. "I've been experimenting with this for long enough. I think it's time for a taste."

"You have been experimenting with a wine and you actually think you're going to make me your guinea pig?" I asked, confused. "Have you not met me before?"

Caden popped the cork out and poured a tiny bit of a sparkling golden wine into the two glasses.

"Before you start arguing with me, I just need you to try it."

I sighed. "Caden, look. I appreciate what you do, pal. I really do. However, I've come to the realization that wine just isn't in the cards for me. I can't stand the stuff."

Caden held out the glass for me.

"That's why I want you to try this. I've tried to create a recipe that'll cater to both the connoisseur and haters of wine alike. You're perfect for this. If you drink this, and you like it, then it'll give me hope that we can try to lure in the non-wine-loving crowd for the next holiday season."

I eyed the wine glass and was silent as I considered.

"Come on, Zack. You're a winery owner. The only way you're going to start liking wine is if you keep trying it."

I grumbled a response not fit for print and took the glass. I clinked it with Caden's and cautiously took a sip. My winemaster watched me like a hawk.

Surprisingly, the liquid that hit my taste buds wasn't too bad. What I was tasting was a complex mix of flavors. I could taste honey, spice, and exotic fruits. With surprise etched all over my face, I stared at my empty glass. This was wine? I had to admit, it wasn't half bad.

Caden was gloating.

"See? I knew you'd like it! This is awesome, Zack! If I can come up with a bottle of wine that even a hater like you could enjoy, then just think of the possibilities!"

"What kind of wine is it?" I asked, curious.

"It's made from botrytis affected grapes," Caden slowly and carefully explained. He poured a tiny bit more into his own glass and held up the bottle, questioningly. He poured some more into my glass once I shrugged and nodded. "You have no idea how big this is. I just poured you a refill. Of wine!"

"It kinda has a sweet taste to it," I decided, after I took another sip. "And why are you only giving me a thimbleful at a time? Is that all you have of it?"

"It's a dessert wine," Caden explained. "You're supposed to have a tiny amount. So it's official? You like it?"

"Hell hath officially frozen over," I muttered as I stared at my empty wine glass. "I will admit it. You came up with a recipe that I'd willingly drink. So, how'd you do it? What's the secret?"

"The secret is the botrytis affected grapes."

"You said that before," I pointed out. "What does that mean?"

I watched Caden take a deep breath. There was something he was hesitant to tell me, I decided. I set down the glass, stooped to give both dogs a pat on the head, and then deliberately—and slowly—crossed my arms over my chest.

"Out with it, amigo. What is it you don't want to tell me?"

"Botrytis is a necrotrophic fungus that can affect many plant species. It's prevalent in wet or humid conditions that have a chance of drying out in a fairly rapid fashion. You may recall we had a very odd summer."

I stopped paying attention after I heard the magic word. Fungus. Wasn't that another name for mold?

"Where'd I lose you?" Caden asked, mistaking my silence for confusion.

"You didn't lose me. I was focusing on the 'fungus' you mentioned. You made this wine with mold? Are you insane?"

"Now, before you completely freak out on me," Caden hurriedly said, "I feel I should remind you that you enjoyed the wine. I saw it with my own eyes."

"If you want to be certain I don't get sick, you'd better explain to me how moldy grapes is not a bad thing. And I do advise you to hurry."

"Mold on grapes is typically a bad thing," Caden agreed. "However, the right mold can be a blessing in disguise."

"And you're telling me that's what we have here?"

Caden nodded. "Since Abigail pestered her mother to the point of the winery being neglected, grapes were allowed to sit on the vine longer than they should have. I found a patch of vines covered with botrytis cinerea. It's a fungus that typically surrounds the grape and causes it to shrivel, thereby leaching out most of the grape's liquid. What's left is an extra sweet pulp that winemakers would then press to extract the remaining liquid. That, my friend, is what you sampled."

"Moldy grapes," I grumbled. I looked down at the dogs. Both Sherlock and Watson were staring expectantly at Caden, as if they were waiting for a treat. "I should sic the dogs on you."

"But you liked it," Caden reminded me. "So it can't be that bad, can it?"

"How many shriveled grapes did it take to make that bottle?"

"Well, it's not just the juice," Caden began. "I also added…"

"How many?" I interrupted. I knew if I didn't stop Caden from launching into a full-fledged explanation of the intricacies of wine-making then I'd literally go gray waiting for him to stop.

"That's the stickler," Caden admitted. "Noble rot wines take a lot of grapes in order to make a single bottle. That's why you'll find most brands are super expensive. I'm thinking we could get away with charging at least $100 a bottle for this. What do you think?"

"Dude, that's cheaper than the Syrah."

Caden blinked at me a few times, "Huh? That's not true. Full retail of the Syrah is listed at around $49 a bottle."

"I was at a restaurant yesterday that was charging $149 a bottle."

Caden didn't seem surprised. He shrugged.

"Think about Disneyland. For the price of a single bottle of water there you could buy an entire case of water at a grocery store."

I had to concede the point. Whatever. If a restaurant wanted to charge that much for one of my bottles of wine, and people were willing to pay for it, then so be it.

"So are you okay with adding this to our lineup?" Caden asked.

"As long as you don't call it 'noble rot'," I said.

"But that's what type of wine it is," Caden insisted.

"Can't we call it something else?" I asked.

"Like what?" Caden wanted to know.

"I don't know. Give it something simple, like a one word name."

"You got it. Thanks, Zack. That's all I needed today."

Caden turned around to head back to the front door when I stopped him.

"Listen, do you know if we have any extra cases of the Syrah lying around? I kinda promised the owner of the restaurant yesterday that I'd do what I can to replenish his stock. He claims he's been calling and that he hasn't been able to get ahold of anyone."

Caden held up the winery's only registered cell phone.

"This is the only number listed on our invoices. I keep this thing with me at all times. I know I haven't missed any calls. Hmm. I only have one person going straight to voice mail, and that's Chateau Restaurant & Wine Bar. I don't suppose it was them, was it?"

I laughed. "Yep. Mr. Dubois. He's the owner. Why do you have him going to voice mail?"

Caden sighed. "Because he won't shut up. When that man gets a burr up his backside, he won't let it go. Contrary to what he might think, the rest of us are not on this planet to jump whenever he snaps his fingers."

"Can you spare a case or two for him? Just this once?"

Caden nodded. "Sure. For you and you alone. I'm not doing this for him. I'll take care of it."

My cell rang. A quick glance at the display confirmed it was Vance. I made sure the leashes were clipped on the dogs and then followed Caden outside.

"Hey, Vance. How's it…"

"We found it!" Vance interrupted. "And it's all thanks to Sherlock!"

"Remind me again what Sherlock found?" I asked as I locked the winery's door. I stopped for a second to admire the heavy duty, bump-proof dead bolt now securing Lentari Cellars from unwanted intruders.

"We found the van!"

My eyebrows shot up.

"Seriously? That's awesome! Who was driving? Was it someone from PV?"

"They haven't pulled him over yet. They've been discreetly following him for the better part of three hours now."

"What? Why?"

"We're trying to catch him red-handed, Zack."

"Ah. And I take it you haven't had much luck yet?"

"Nope. Not yet. All he's doing is driving around, delivering packages."

"Did you get a license plate number? Who's it registered to?"

"The van is registered to a Charlie Sumner. He's an employee of a shipping company based out of Portland. Sumner is stationed in a satellite office in Medford."

"A shipping company," I repeated. "Do you believe them?"

"Actually? Yes. I think the company is legit. However, I think the driver is dirty as anything."

"Have you guys been able to check out his tire tracks yet?" I asked.

"No. He hasn't driven through any mud, or water, or anything else that'll leave a track. So we have several cars keeping an eye on him, waiting to jump in should he do something stupid. Or leave tracks. Whatever."

"So how long are you going to give him?"

"Probably not too much longer," Vance admitted with a sigh. "All we need him to do is … Zack? Let me call you back. Jones is calling me. He's one of the officers that's tailing him."

Vance signed off just as I made it back to the house. I was considering going for a drive when my cell rang ten minutes later.

"Hey Vance, that was quick."

"We got him."

"Sorry? What was that?"

"Jones tailed the suspect to a quiet residential neighborhood, watched him get out of his van, and approach a house. Zack, they arrested him after he was spotted peering through the windows. They've just brought him to the station and they've also impounded the van. I thought you might like to watch the interview."

I glanced over at the dogs. Both had jumped up on the couch and were stretching out in preparation for an afternoon nap. I turned on the television and set it to the Animal Planet station.

Don't laugh. My dogs enjoy watching television. I don't know what that says about me, but if I could use modern technology as an impromptu dog sitter, then so be it. I left the dogs on the couch and made my way to the police station. The cop at the front desk was one of the policemen who had admitted they were fans of Sherlock. I was promptly waved through. I saw Vance talking with several other cops. He looked up, waved me over, and together we stepped inside the observational part of the interrogation room.

"Is that the Grinch?" I asked, looking at the young teenager sitting by himself in the room. He was probably eighteen or nineteen, had the unhealthy look of someone who didn't eat too well, and was fidgeting on his seat. He looked more annoyed than scared. "He doesn't look like much of a thief. Or a murderer, for that matter. Are you sure that's our guy?"

"Look at him," Vance said, turning to look at the kid. "He's not afraid, or concerned. This is someone that has been in an interrogation room before."

"I will definitely say that it's much more fun to be on this side of the mirror," I said. "I don't know how that kid is staying so calm. I certainly didn't enjoy sitting by myself in there. Wait. Is that what you were doing to me back when I had been arrested? You were all in here waiting for me to crack?"

Vance managed to keep his face comfortably parked in neutral.

"Okay, that's long enough. It's time to find out what this guy knows."

"You didn't answer my question," I called out as Vance left the room. Before the door could swing all the way shut, I watched a hand insert itself inside the room and pull the door back open. Captain Nelson appeared. He nodded at me and sank down into the closest chair.

"Have I missed anything?" the captain asked me.

"No. Vance just left to go talk to him."

"Think he did it?" the captain casually asked.

I turned to look at the man who once thought I was guilty of murder and had no qualms about holding me in jail until a better culprit could be found. Since when had he been this chatty? I found his demeanor strangely disquieting.

"I wish I knew," I said.

"Guess," the captain instructed.

"Well, speaking from experience back when I was sitting in that seat, I could tell you that I was uncomfortable as all get-out. I didn't want to be there. I didn't know how to convince you people that I was innocent. It was frustrating."

"Go on," Captain Nelson said as a smile formed on his face.

"This kid is looking around the room as though he thinks it could use a fresh coat of paint. He doesn't appear to be nervous. Oh, don't get me wrong, he doesn't want to be there. I don't know if I can say that he knows why he's been brought in. My first reaction is that, no, he didn't do it. Then again, this could all be an act."

"So you think he's innocent," the captain casually asked.

"You asked," I reminded him. "I answered."

"Not bad, Anderson. You'd make a fair detective."

We watched Vance enter the room, drop the file on the table, and pull out a chair.

"Good afternoon, Mr. Sumner. How are you doing today?"

"Not so good," I heard the teenager say. "Why am I in here? I'm going to be fired if I don't get my deliveries done."

"On a Sunday?" Vance skeptically asked. "Not even the Post Office delivers on a Sunday. What's the matter, Charlie? Falling behind on your deliveries because you found something else to do?"

The teenager hung his head and fell silent.

Vance nodded. "That's what I thought. So, why don't you tell me what happened. From the beginning."

"I shouldn't have done it, okay? It was wrong and I was stupid."

Vance pulled out a pen and a pad of paper. He slid

them over to the kid. When Charlie refused to look up, Vance rapped his knuckles on the table. Charlie flinched, as though he had been struck on the arm.

"Go ahead and write everything down," Vance instructed, pointing at the notepad. "Use your own words. We need to have it on record."

"I was set up," Charlie all but whispered.

"What was that?" Vance asked, looking up. "What did you say?"

"Those sons of bitches set me up," Charlie muttered again, raising his voice. "They told me it'd be the perfect way to score some extra cash."

"By breaking into people's houses and stealing their Christmas presents?" Vance asked. "What kind of a lame-brain lowlife would do that to someone else? Especially at this time of year?"

"What are you talking about?" Charlie demanded. "I didn't break into any houses."

"Of course you didn't," Vance sighed. "You're telling me that it's just a coincidence that your van is spotted outside two crime scenes?"

"I don't know what you're talking about," Charlie insisted. "I was never at any crime scene, just a demolition zone."

"What was that?" Vance repeated, confused.

"What was that?" I asked, turning to the captain for confirmation. Captain Nelson looked just as puzzled as I did.

"I said, I was only at a demolition zone. They said the stuff was just going to be thrown away. It'd be a great way to sell it cheaply and make a few bucks. What's the harm in that?"

"What demolition zone are you referring to?" Vance asked. "I know of only one in PV. Are you talking about the Square L?"

Charlie's head fell again.

"Interesting," Captain Nelson mused. "Sounds like the kid was helping himself to whatever had been left inside that convenience store. I'm not sure I buy it."

"Neither do I," I told the captain.

"You're telling me," Vance was saying, "that you're admitting to robbing the Square L? When it had already been closed?"

Charlie nodded and sulked.

"I wonder how he got in," I mused aloud. "It's not like they'd leave the door unlocked."

Captain Nelson rose from his feet, grabbed the old-fashioned microphone that was sitting on the table in front of us, and punched a button.

"Ask him how he got inside the store."

"So how did you get inside the store?" Vance asked, almost immediately after the captain had set the mic back down.

"Umm, I found an unlocked door?"

Vance had the kid's file open in front of him. He had been busy scribbling notes. He looked up and fixed the kid with a stare.

"Really? That's the story you're sticking with?"

Much to my surprise, Charlie grew angry.

"Listen, I don't know why you're fixating on me, 'cause I didn't do anything, but the longer I stay in here the more likely I am to get fired. You may not care about that, but I sure do. I can't afford to lose my job. So do what you need to do. Ask away. The sooner you do, the sooner you'll see that you've got the wrong guy."

Surprised, I turned to see what the captain thought of that. Unsurprisingly, Captain Nelson was frowning. Could he think that they have the wrong guy, too?

"He sure sounds confident," I observed.

"Too confident," the captain agreed. He picked up the mic again. "Ask him about his tires."

I saw Vance glance up at the mirror. He nodded. He made a few more notes in the file before he looked back at Charlie.

"Tell me about your tires."

"My tires?" Charlie repeated, confused. "What about them?"

"We need to know the make, manufacturer, and size."

"I honestly have no idea," Charlie admitted. "I bought whatever was on sale."

"What's the make and model of your van?" Vance asked.

"It's a 2004 Ford Econoline," Charlie answered.

"Do you do much off-roading in your van?" Vance asked.

"Nice question," I heard the captain say.

"Off-roading? No. Why do you ask?"

"You have all-terrain tires on your van. It's a legitimate question, Mr. Sumner."

Charlie shrugged. "I sometimes have to drive in the snow. I told the salesman at the tire store that I needed something that could handle all types of weather. That's what he recommended. Sure, there were tires that could perform better but it was all I could afford."

The door opened to the observation room. Both the captain and I turned at the intrusion.

"I'm sorry to bother you, Captain," an officer was

saying. His name tag identified him as Stidwell. "I thought you'd like to know. We just received the report on the tires."

"And?" Captain Nelson asked as he reached out to take the proffered report.

Stidwell grinned. "It's a match, captain."

"Excellent. Thank you, Stidwell. That'll be all."

Captain Nelson picked up the mic.

"The report is in. The tires are a match."

I watched a smile reminiscent of the Cheshire cat spread across Vance's face. He looked at Charlie and cocked his head. The kid immediately became nervous.

"What? Why are you looking at me like that?"

"Care to tell me…"

"I'm coming in," Captain Nelson said into the microphone, interrupting Vance in mid-sentence.

"Your day is about to become a lot worse," Vance told the kid.

"What?" Charlie stammered. "How could it possibly get worse?"

The door opened, admitting Captain Nelson. He tossed the report up onto the table. Vance opened the folder and skimmed through the single sheet of paper found within.

"What is that?" Charlie nervously asked.

"It's a lab report. We asked our lab boys to compare the photos from the crime scenes to the tires on your van. They're a match, kid. We can now place your van at two of the three burglaries that have happened in our city."

"My van was nowhere near your burglaries!" Charlie cried. "You have the wrong guy!"

"You're going to be charged with breaking and entering, which is typically a misdemeanor…" Captain Nelson was saying.

"Usually results in jail time of less than a year," Vance

idly mentioned as he twirled a pen in his fingers.

"And three cases of breaking and entering with the intent to commit a felony…" the captain continued.

"That'd be a felony," Vance added, "which will usually mean you get prison time of more than a year."

"And one count of voluntary manslaughter," Captain Nelson finished. He hadn't broken eye contact with the suspect, even though Charlie was now refusing to look anyone in the eye, as though he had lost attention. However, as soon as the captain brought up the manslaughter charge, Charlie's attention rapidly came back to him.

"Manslaughter? What the f… I didn't kill anyone! You've gotta believe me!"

"Then convince us otherwise," Vance said. His voice had dropped and had become completely emotionless. "Evidence suggests you are the killer. You say you're not? Prove it. Where were you last Tuesday?"

"Last Tuesday?" Charlie repeated. "I don't know. I don't remember."

"You were obviously in town," Vance remarked. He yawned, as though this interrogation was boring him to tears. He tapped the police report in front of him. "I've got proof right here that you were. Would you care to explain that?"

"I work out of Medford," Charlie hastily explained. "My father gave me his old van. RMS Shipping was hiring, and the one stipulation they had was that you had your own vehicle. So, I applied. I've made hundreds of deliveries in both Medford and Pomme Valley. You know what? You said you wanted to know where I was on Tuesday. Check my logs. RMS makes me keep a detailed log of everywhere I go. I have to note the address, my odometer readings, everything. That'll prove to you that I was nowhere near your burglaries."

"Do you even know where those burglaries occurred?" Vance asked.

"Well, no," Charlie admitted.

"We've sent for your delivery logs," Captain Nelson told the kid. "One way or the other, we'll know where you've been."

Charlie nodded. "Good. Then you'll see this is all one big mistake."

The door opened inside my viewing room. A cop poked his head in. It was Stidwell.

"Where's the captain?" he asked me.

I wordlessly pointed at the occupants inside the interrogation room.

Officer Stidwell grabbed the mic from the counter and pressed the button.

"We have the delivery logs. They do show that the kid was making deliveries Tuesday at the time of the break-in. We're checking with the residences where he claims to have been."

I watched Captain Nelson briefly flick his eyes over to the window. He nodded. Then he tapped his watch.

"Yes, sir," Stidwell said. "We'll let you know what we find out and we'll hurry."

Captain Nelson nodded again.

Thirty minutes later found me still sitting in my chair, watching the antics in the interrogation room. Vance was still asking the same questions, over and over, although he was rephrasing each question just a little bit differently from the previous one. Maybe it was a police tactic? Perhaps it was a technique to extract information from a suspect?

Keep asking the same thing over and over and perhaps eventually you'll catch the suspect in a slip of the tongue.

I didn't know how much longer I was going to wait inside that stuffy room. As far as I could tell, Vance and the captain were no closer to getting a confession out of the kid than they were when they first started. Charlie was maintaining his innocence and no matter how many times Vance asked the question, the suspect insisted he had nothing to do with any robberies and most especially the murder.

The door opened again. Stidwell was back. This time, unfortunately, his face was grim. He sat down at the table with a sigh and punched a finger down on the button.

"Captain? Stidwell here. We've verified all the kid's deliveries. They check out. Every single one of them. We even checked on Monday and again on last Friday. Every recipient confirmed the delivery driver was polite and cordial. Service with a smile, they said."

I looked at Captain Nelson. He was frowning again. He nudged Vance on the shoulder and inclined his head toward the door. Both of them exited the room and came hurrying inside the observation room.

"What is it?" Vance was saying. "What's up?"

"The kid's story checks out," Captain Nelson told him.

"It's true," Stidwell confirmed. "Everybody we talked to said the kid was pleasant to be around. They could even confirm the times."

"That means the kid is innocent, right?" I asked.

All three cops turned to look at me as if they just noticed that a civilian was present.

"His alibis have checked out, true," Vance admitted, "but we cannot ignore the evidence. Those tires were at the scene of both crimes."

"Unless there's another vehicle driving around with the exact same tires," Stidwell suggested.

"I'm not letting this guy go," Captain Nelson stated. "I can hold him for twenty-four hours." He looked up at the clock on the wall. "That gives you less than twenty-two hours, Detective. Find me a smoking gun or else I have to cut him loose. I don't need to remind you how much I don't like open cases."

Vance nodded. He gave me an inscrutable look and automatically headed toward the door. I followed. Just as we walked by the front desk, a commotion sounded from behind us.

"What's that all about?" I asked, turning to look back down the hallway toward the interrogation room we had just exited.

"I'm not sure," Vance admitted. "Stay here. I'll find out."

Five minutes later Vance was back. And he was out of breath.

"We ... we have the wrong guy, Zack."

"How do you know?" I asked.

"Because there's been a fourth burglary!"

NINE

Monday morning found me pacing the confines of Cookbook Nook while I waited for Vance to call. Yes, there had been another burglary, but I had been told that the dogs and I wouldn't be allowed to step foot inside the crime scene until all the evidence had been processed. In layman's terms, it meant that the PVPD had to say they've collected every feasible bit of evidence before they'd allow me on scene.

I eyed the clock up on the wall behind Jillian's register. It had been over twelve hours since the call came in last night. Clearly the PVPD wasn't taking any chances this time and were doing as thorough an investigation as possible.

Nothing will make you look bad like bragging to the general public that you have a 'person of interest' in the case and yet another burglary happens right under your noses. I chuckled and shook my head. Talk about poor timing. The mayor had literally been in the middle of his town meeting when he had been notified about the burglary. To say he was less than amused would have been an understatement.

So, while I waited for permission to take the dogs to the crime scene, I was killing time in Jillian's shop. And, I have to tell you, it was a real eye-opener. Having never worked in retail before, I could only gawk at Jillian and her staff. She had confided in me that she usually only has four or five employees on her payroll, but during the holiday season, it wouldn't be surprising to see that number swell to over a dozen.

Her store was hopping.

People were lining up, waiting to make their purchases. Customers would then ask about certain recipes, at which Jillian would point them to the correct cookbook, all without batting an eye. If someone asked where a specific kitchen utensil could be found, then Jillian could not only pinpoint exactly where it was in the store, but also instruct them on how to properly use the item. And, nine times out of ten, she could typically tell the customer how to do the job better with a completely different utensil.

The people loved her. She was knowledgeable and it showed. Jillian worked the registers, answered questions, and replenished stock whenever a hole appeared on any of her shelves or displays.

"We just sold our last Kitchen Helper mixer on the floor," I heard one of the girls say to Jillian.

"The pink one?" Jillian asked, turning to the girl.

"Yes. I didn't think that one would ever sell."

"Welcome to the final Christmas rush. Do we have any

more left in the back?"

The girl nodded. "I think so. It's not pink, though. I think it might be stainless steel."

"That'll do."

"Are any of the carts available?" the girl asked. "It's too heavy for me to lift."

I watched Jillian scan the store, looking for one of the store's two push carts that she used to haul books and heavy items from one end of the store to the other. Before she could locate one, however, her eyes locked on me and she smiled. I had just sat down in one of the comfy arm chairs Jillian had set up in a reading area when I noticed I was being watched. Right about that time both dogs stretched out on the thick rug and sighed contentedly.

"Do you need something?" I asked.

"Would you mind giving Cassie a hand? We need to move a few mixers from the storeroom to the front area."

"Sure," I said, rising to my feet. I looked down at the dogs. "Wait here, guys. I'll be right back."

Sherlock promptly yawned and closed his eyes. Watson looked like she was moments away from joining him. I looked up to see Jillian still watching me.

"I'll keep an eye on them. If I see them move, then I'll offer them a t-r-e-a-t."

I've always heard people spell words around dogs. Back then, I had thought it was a pointless waste of time. Now, however, I totally understand. Anyone who owns a dog knows there are certain words you just don't say aloud. Treat, ride, and walk being three of the most popular.

"She must really like you," Cassie quietly informed me as I followed her into the back storeroom.

"Oh? Why do you say that?"

"Not only is she planning on having the store closed on Christmas, but she's also planning on closing the store on Christmas Eve, too."

I felt my face flaming up.

"Why do you think I had anything to do with that?"

Cassie turned to look at me with an incredulous look.

"Because she talks about you all the time. And your dogs, too. I love your dogs. They're so cute!"

"Dare I ask what she's said about me?" I asked as I picked up the box that she had indicated.

"Just that she enjoys spending so much time with you," Cassie wistfully said. "It's so nice to see. Don't you dare hurt her."

Surprised, I looked over the large bulky box and saw the teenager giving me a stern look.

"Have no fear. I won't ever hurt her. And I think it's nice that you're looking out for her."

"She's done a lot for me," Cassie told me, as she held the doors open leading back out to the showroom. "I've worked for her for several years now. And I will tell you that this is the first year that I'm aware of that Jillian has said she has no plans on coming in on Christmas day."

"That might change," I chuckled.

Cassie stopped so suddenly that I almost ran into her.

"Why would you say something like that?"

I smiled. "No, let me explain. My parents are coming for Christmas. She might be spending more time here than you think. And you know what? I'd keep her company."

Cassie laughed and indicated a spot on the floor in front of an empty section of shelving. I set the box down, helped unpack the shiny new stainless steel mixer, and volunteered to return the box to the storeroom. I checked on the dogs and was pleased to see that both were still in their down positions. In fact, both dogs were fast asleep.

Not long afterward, the morning rush passed and I was delighted to see Jillian heading my way, holding a mug of hot tea. She gave me a questioning look and held up her mug. I shook my head no. Tea. Blech.

"So what did you think of the town meeting last night?" I companionably asked her as she sipped her tea.

"Bad timing," Jillian decided after a moment's hesitation. "I actually felt bad for the mayor."

Bad timing was an understatement. The mayor had been nearly an hour into his scheduled town meeting. He had been fielding questions from concerned citizens left and right. He had handled himself with poise and dignity. I'm told that the people were visibly starting to relax. Nothing, it would seem, helped calm frayed nerves better than hearing about the police had a suspect in custody. Everything was going precisely as planned.

And that's when the proverbial doggie doo hit the fan.

As I was saying, about an hour into the town meeting one of the reporters must have been sent a text from an editor with a police scanner, because out of the blue the reporter wanted to know what the mayor thought about the most recent burglary. When the mayor started in with what had to be a scripted speech about how sorry he was to hear about the dreadful murder happening in their beloved city, he became understandably flustered when the reporter mentioned that this was from earlier in the day. After they had taken their suspect into custody.

Questions were bandied about. Voices were raised. Shouts erupted. The mayor tried to regain control of the crowd but anyone could see that he was now fighting a losing battle. His aides ushered him away from the melee as the police arrived on the scene.

From what I've been told, the mayor placed a none-too-pleasant phone call to Captain Nelson and probably ripped him a new one. It would also explain why the naturally photogenic police captain deliberately avoided anyone with a camera or microphone. That was also why every single policeman and policewoman had been called into active duty.

The owner of the home where the fourth burglary had taken place was given lodging at one of the nearby hotels. The home owner, one of only two lawyers who called PV home, had agreed to vacate the house while the forensic team went through everything with a fine-tooth comb.

"So, do you think the police have arrested the wrong man?" Jillian asked, breaking me out of my reverie.

"As much as I hate to admit it, I think they have. I'm not convinced that the guy with the van is our culprit."

"Why do you say that?" Jillian asked.

"Well, first off, all of his alibis have checked out. Vance told me that they've checked every single delivery that kid has made since last Wednesday. Everything checks out. Then, there are the tires."

"I thought the police said that it was a match?"

"They did," I said, nodding. "However, the report only said that both sets of tracks were made by the same make of tire. A closer examination of the van's tires confirms that the tires on his van are too new. The tire tracks at the crime scenes show more wear on the tread."

"What did Vance say they were going to do now?" Jillian asked.

I shrugged. "I don't know. He didn't say. I feel bad for

the guy. This is no way to spend the holidays. I can only hope that Sherlock finds something else when we're finally allowed into the house."

My cell phone started ringing just then. I fished it out of my pocket, glanced at the display, and groaned. I turned it around so that Jillian could see it.

"You'd better answer that," Jillian warned, giving me a frown.

"Hey, Mom. What's up?"

"Zachary! How good of you to answer your phone!"

"Have I ever not answered it?" I asked, adding my own frown to the mix.

"Why, yes, come to think of it."

"We'll table that argument for another time," I jovially told her. For some reason I was anxious to prove to Jillian that I could get along with my parents. "What can I do for you, Mom?"

"You can tell me where you are."

"Where I am? I'm in Pomme Valley, Mom. Where else would I be?"

"But where specifically?"

"I'm out and about. I had some errands to run. Why? Where are you?"

"Having coffee at a place called Wired Coffee & Café. It's quite nice in here."

I'm sure my face drained of all color. They were at the coffee shop here in town? That meant they were presently only a few doors down, off of Oregon Street! What! They weren't supposed to be here for another week! My sneaky mother must have hit the road the instant she decided she was planning on coming to PV for Christmas. Shitshitshit!

"What's the matter?" Jillian asked me in a hushed voice,

concerned. "Your face has gone completely pale."

While my mother began to regale me with her adventures on the open road with my father, I muted the phone and gave Jillian an alarmed look.

"They're here."

Jillian's eyebrows shot up, surprised.

"I thought they wouldn't be here for another few days."

"That makes two of us," I grumbled. "They're already here in town."

Jillian smiled. "Really? Where are they?"

"Just down the street at Wired. I can't believe they're already here. I haven't even had a chance to clean the house yet."

"Well, invite them over."

"Here?" I sputtered. "Now? Words cannot begin to describe what a bad idea that is."

"Why?" Jillian innocently asked. "You have nothing to hide. I have nothing to hide. And besides, I'd like to meet your parents."

"I don't think you truly understand the gravity of the situation," I began.

"Zachary Anderson, either you tell your mother where we presently are or else I'm walking straight to Wired and will escort them here myself."

"I sure hope you know what you're doing," I muttered, as I unmuted my phone.

My mother was still going on and on about how cars nowadays were way too complicated to learn how to use. Evidently, my mother had traded in her old Buick and splurged for a new Acura ILX.

"Mom? Mom! Hey, take a breath, okay? I'll tell you where I am. We're not far from where you presently are.

Yes, you heard me right. I said we. Yes, she's here, too. Her name? Her name is Jillian. Look, I know you have questions, but why not just ask them in person? Come on down to her store. That's where we are right now." I muted the phone one more time and gave Jillian an imploring look. "This is your last chance to get out of this."

Jillian laughed and swatted my arm.

"So where are you?" my mother asked me again.

I sighed and unmuted the phone.

"I'm at a store called Cookbook Nook. It's…"

"…the big purple building we passed on the way in!" my mother finished for me. "We'll be right there!"

I hung up the phone and looked down at the dogs. Sherlock, sensing he was being watched, looked up at me and cocked his head. Watson also had opened her sleepy eyes and was watching me closely.

"Man your battle stations, guys. We're going to have company."

Two minutes later, they arrived. My mother, a short woman with curly, short, unnatural auburn hair, appeared in the doorway. She was wearing a full winter coat complete with a brown wooly scarf wrapped securely around her neck. And, just in case there was someone in the vicinity who hadn't pegged her as a tourist, my mother was wearing gloves and a set of ear muffs.

My father was holding the door open for my mother. I had received my height from him, which meant he was a solid six feet tall. If I wasn't mistaken, it looked like my father's hair was even more gray than I remembered it. Perhaps my absence had something to do with it?

I hoped not.

"Zachary! There you are!"

My mother rushed forward to encompass me in a full bear hug. I'm certain she would have not broken the hug if not for the warning woofs Sherlock directed at her. Surprised, my mother looked down at the corgis, as if noticing them for the first time. Who knows? Maybe she was.

"I recognize you from the other night!" my mother said as she squatted down to give Sherlock a friendly pat on the head. "Oh, look, William! There are the dogs! Aren't they the sweetest things?"

My mother's voice had risen in pitch and had taken on an undertone of sheer giddiness. In essence, it was corgi-speak for, 'I want to be a member of your fan club, so you can trust me'. Sherlock's ears went down, his butt started wiggling, and he whined. He wanted to be released so he could go welcome the newest member of his pack.

My father stepped up to me and shook my hand

"Glad to see you, boy. How have you been?"

"Good, Dad. Thanks. Listen, you two, I've got someone I'd like you to meet. Mom, Dad, I'd like you to meet Jillian Cooper, owner and operator of Cookbook Nook. Jillian? These are my parents. This is William Anderson, my father, and Dana Anderson, my mother."

Jillian smiled and offered them her hand.

"It's a pleasure to finally meet you both. You must be so proud of Zachary for moving all the way out here and running such a successful winery."

"I've heard a lot of good things about Lentari Cellars," my father returned, giving Jillian's hand a formal shake. "I can't wait to try the wines."

My mother, being five-foot-two, looked up at Jillian and gave her a guarded smile. I deliberately stepped in front of my mother, effectively blocking Jillian from her view. I pointed at a nearby rack of books.

"Let me show you around, Mom. Jillian? Would you mind?"

Jillian managed to hide her smile before she turned away. Thankfully, I could tell that she knew I wanted a private word with my mother and I didn't want any witnesses.

"Before you say anything," my mother began, "I should let you know I have a right to make sure my son is okay."

"By showing up a week early and giving Jillian a less-than-enthusiastic smile? Come on, Mom. If I noticed, then you'd better believe she noticed it, too."

"I just want you to be happy, Zachary," my mother protested.

"And I am. I actually didn't think I could be after Sam's death. So I need you to listen to me now. Do not try to psychoanalyze her in any way shape or form. No trick questions, no puzzles, and no asking her about her family unless she brings it up first."

"Really, Zachary," my mother exclaimed. "Do you really think so low of me?"

"Promise me, Mom."

"Fine. I promise."

"Good," I nodded, as we headed back to Jillian and Dad. "I'll consider the matter dropped. Now, tell me. Why'd you guys come a week early? Were you trying to see how dirty my house is before I have a chance to clean it?"

My father laughed.

"I tried to tell your mother that we should give you a fair warning we were on the road. She wouldn't hear of it."

"Awwooooo!"

The three of us turned to see Sherlock still holding his 'sit'. I had yet to release him and he was making it known that he wanted his turn in the introductions. I looked at my mom and smiled. I smelled a little payback.

"Mom, Sherlock wants to be introduced. He and Watson like to be included when it comes to meeting new people."

"Your dogs want to meet us?" my father incredulously asked. "And for the record, I love their names."

I pointed at two of the recliners in the reading area in the middle of Jillian's store.

"Perhaps you two should be sitting down for this."

My mom was wearing the best confused expression I have ever seen on her face as she hesitantly lowered herself into a recliner. My father plunked down in a nearby chair moments later. I walked over to Sherlock, laid an arm across his shoulder, and grinned at my parents.

"Ready to be introduced in proper corgi fashion?"

"Umm, sure," my father slowly said.

"Mom? You ready?"

"They're just dogs, Zachary. What is it you think they're going to do?"

I gave Sherlock a gentle nudge. "Are you ready, boy?"

Sherlock gave another low howl. His front end started bouncing. His butt wiggled and he crouched low, as though he was about ready to take on the hundred meter dash. My father's eyes narrowed and a smile formed on his face. I could tell he knew what was about to happen.

"Sherlock, Watson … release!"

The tri-color corgi made it over to my mother's chair in 0.3 seconds. He leapt up onto her lap with a single bound and before anyone knew what was happening, he was covering her face with corgi kisses.

"Aaauuugh! What is he…? No, don't lick the insides of my mouth! Ugh!"

My father laughed as he watched the onslaught of corgi affection. He looked down at little Watson. The red and white corgi had stopped at his feet and was craning her neck to look up at him. My father stretched a hand out to pet her, but was surprised when Watson tried to jump in his lap. However, she didn't get a running start like Sherlock had. All that ended up happening was that she bounced up and down on her back legs.

"Does she want to be picked up?" my father asked.

"Zachary!" my mother cried from her recliner. "Call off your dog!"

Smiling at Sherlock's antics, I ignored my mother and gently picked up Watson to place her on my father's lap. Watson stretched her neck out to give the underside of my father's neck a single lick. Satisfied that proper greetings had been made, Watson laid across my father's lap and watched her pack mate continue to go after my mother's face.

"Seriously, Zachary! Call him off! He's going to lick off all my makeup!"

Jillian came to her rescue. She appeared beside me, holding a familiar bag of doggie treats. The simple process of unsealing the bag caught both of their attention. I caught Sherlock before he could execute a Superman leap off my mother's chair. Watson waited for my father to lower her to the ground before she began to run around Jillian's legs.

"How are you doin', Mom?" I casually asked, throwing her a grin.

"I never imagined such a small dog could be so strong,"

my mother told me, pulling open her purse and reapplying her lipstick. "Or quick. Every time I turned away his face was right there."

Finished with their treats, the corgis returned to my side and watched my parents with speculative eyes. If I didn't know any better, then I'd say Sherlock liked the taste of my mother's makeup. I swear he was ready to jump back up on her lap for round two. Watson, on the other hand, kept staring at me, then at my father, and then back at me.

"She must think you're Zachary," Jillian explained to my father. "Look at the way she keeps looking between you two. She probably can't figure it out."

"I don't recall ever liking a dog as much as I like that one," my father admitted. He stooped to hold out a hand. Watson immediately came over to give his hand a lick. "Are all corgis like this?"

I pointed at Sherlock, "You did see what he just did to Mom, right?"

"You are going to make a dog lover out of me, little girl," my father affectionately told Watson.

What did she do in return? Promptly hit the ground to roll onto her back. My father then proceeded to give her a belly rub.

"You've made a friend for life," I told my dad.

"So aside from making wine," my dad said, straightening up, "what else have you been doing around here? What do you like to do for fun?"

I thought of the recent run of burglaries. I thought back to when I chased a kid dressed as a mummy a few months ago. Then, of course, I couldn't forget the first time I stepped foot in Pomme Valley. I had been arrested for murder less than twenty-four hours later.

"Oh, nothing much. It gets kinda boring around here, but you know what? Most people like it that way."

Vance couldn't have timed it better. My cell began to ring. The icing on the cake was the fact that I had put my money where my mouth was and had purchased a custom ring tone for my detective friend. You're a Mean One, Mr. Grinch, began playing on my phone. I groaned and hastily silenced my phone just as fast as I could.

"Excuse me," I apologized to my parents and smiled at Jillian. "I need to take this. Hey, Vance, what's up?"

"They're ready for you, buddy. And let me say that I certainly hope Sherlock finds something."

How was I going to explain this to my parents?

"What does Sherlock need to find?" my father asked, confused.

I groaned again. The store was quiet enough, and the cellular connection was clear enough, so Vance's voice was easily heard by everyone present. I looked over at Jillian, who shrugged helplessly.

"Who's there with you?"

"My parents drove up—from Phoenix—for Christmas."

"That was nice of them. Sorry to pull you away from your family time, but the fourth burglary scene has finally been cleared for your arrival."

"We'll be right there."

I sighed, plastered the biggest, dumbest-looking smile I could come up on my face, and turned to my parents.

"So, listen. Something's come up and I need to, uh, that is … I need to…"

"Go to the scene of a burglary?" my father curiously asked. "Did we all hear that right? Why would your friend want you to go to the scene of a crime?"

"That was Vance," Jillian helpfully supplied. "He's a detective for the PVPD."

"Why would he want your help?" my mother suspiciously asked.

"Believe it or not, he doesn't," I cryptically answered. "Jillian, I am truly sorry. I hesitate to do this, but I have to go."

Jillian smiled at me, "We'll be just fine, Zachary. Go help Vance."

"He'll be leaving the dogs, right?" I heard my father hopefully ask Jillian.

"Actually, the dogs will be going with him," Jillian answered. "Can I offer the two of you a hot beverage? I know you just came from a coffee shop, but if you'd like a refill then we can head upstairs to the café."

My mother looked at me with a guarded expression before she turned to Jillian, smiled graciously, and slipped her arm through Jillian's.

"Why, that'd be lovely. Come on, William. Let's get to know this lovely young lady. And perhaps she can tell us what's been going on with Zachary, since trying to get information out of him is like pulling teeth."

I gathered up the dogs and headed outside. According to the text message Vance just sent me, the fourth burglary had happened on the eastern side of town. In fact, it was within walking distance of the high school. How did I know that? It's because I actually ran through the area in hot pursuit of a fake mummy almost two months ago. As I pulled up to the house, I could see that there were still a few police cars parked nearby.

Vance was waiting for us at the front door of the

house. As I walked up the steps, I decided to reclassify the place from a simple 'house' to a full-fledged manor. This home was huge! I was surprised it didn't have a perimeter gate encircling the entire property with its own guarded entrance.

"Wow," I said as we stepped inside. "Look at this place. It's huge! Who lives here?"

"Mr. and Mrs. Jason Hawkins. Mr. Hawkins is one of two practicing attorneys who calls Pomme Valley home. So whatever you do, Zack, don't screw up. This guy is a high-powered attorney who has offices all across the state."

"Swell," I grumbled. "No pressure there. Come on Sherlock, let's do your thing. Watson? Keep up, okay?"

We slowly walked the ground floor of the Tudor-style mansion. We passed a huge study, a library, at least four bedrooms—each with its own bathroom—a kitchen with acres of granite countertops that would make Martha Stewart green with envy, and a living room that any movie enthusiast would kill for. I hesitated after that last thought. To kill for? That wasn't right. We've already proven that these burglaries are not about the money. One look at this attorney's beautiful home quelled any notion that this was solely motivated by money.

As we approached the living room I was once again led straight to the tree by Sherlock. Both corgis looked up at the tree and cocked their heads, as though they had spotted some cryptic message that only a dog could read. The tree, by the way, was gorgeous. It had to be easily nine feet tall. The scent instantly made me think of horse-drawn sleds being pulled through snow-covered trees. I inhaled a second time and sighed blissfully. Too bad all trees didn't smell like this one. The tree was a deep blue-green color with soft half-inch needles and strong branches. The home owner, it would seem, had decorated the tree with various sized bulbs. The larger four-inch delicate glass bulbs occupied the lower half of the tree while three-inch bulbs were in the middle, and two-inch glass bulbs occupied the top portion of the tree.

"It's just a tree, guys," I groaned. "Let it go, okay?"

"Anything?" Vance hopefully asked, as he appeared by my right elbow.

I shook my head. "He's focusing on the tree again. It's always the darn tree. I don't know why he fixates on some and not on others. I think there's something we're missing here. We're in a different part of town. Maybe we can try doing that experiment again with another tree?"

"There are two more upstairs," a friendly voice suddenly informed us.

Vance and I looked over to see a man younger than I was, and taller, dressed in an impeccable blue suit. He had just put a briefcase down on the couch. He held out a hand.

"Jason Hawkins. And you are?"

"Detective Vance Samuelson."

"Zack Anderson. Oh, sorry. That's Sherlock on my right and Watson standing next to Vance."

Jason smiled down at the corgis.

"So these are the detective dogs I've heard so much about. Hello, Sherlock. Are you friendly?"

The lawyer stooped down to hold out a hand. Sherlock approached first. He gave the lawyer's hand a friendly lick. Watson did the same a few moments later.

"What are you doing back in here, Mr. Hawkins?" Vance asked.

"I was notified that the crime scene techs had left,

indicating they had learned all they were going to. I asked if my family and I could return home. I was told I could. I'm sorry. I wasn't aware there was anyone left in the house. Wait until my kids get a load of this. They love dogs, especially those two."

"Your kids know about Sherlock and Watson?" I asked, amazed.

Jason nodded. "They do. As you may have imagined, I have spent quite a bit of time down at the station. I've seen you there a few times, Mr. Anderson. I then tell my kids about my day and be sure to mention the dogs."

"Did you say something about having more trees elsewhere?" Vance asked.

Jason nodded and pointed at the nearby staircase.

"Yes, sir. On the second floor. You'll actually find two more."

"May we see them, please?" Vance asked.

Jason nodded. "Of course. This way."

We followed the friendly home owner over to the staircase. Both corgis hesitated at the foot of the stairs and stared expectantly up at me. With a sigh, I picked up Watson, who happened to be closest to me. Before Vance could pick up Sherlock, Jason was there.

"May I? My kids will love to hear that I was able to carry the famous little Sherlock in our own house."

I nodded my assent. Sherlock noticed I wasn't the one doing the lifting and turned to see who was carrying him. He studied Jason for a few moments before evidently deciding he was harmless.

Once on the second floor Jason led us to a second—smaller—living room. There was a tree, just as he had indicated. Then he pointed off down a hallway.

"My wife loves Christmas," Jason explained. "There's a four-foot tree in the master bedroom, too."

I looked at the tree. This one wasn't the same as the one downstairs. True, it was only about six feet tall, but the shape was different. The composition of the branches was different. Even the length of the pine needles was different. Holy crap on a cracker. I really was the stupidest thing on two legs. I turned to Vance and hooked a thumb at the tree.

"That's not the same type of tree as the one downstairs."

Vance gave the tree a quick, cursory glance. He shrugged.

"Does it matter? I'm more interested in the fact that there are presents under this tree."

Surprised, I turned to see for myself. Sure enough, a dozen smaller presents were scattered under the tree's canopy. I looked down to see what Sherlock was doing. The corgis were both staring back at the staircase. It would seem they wanted to go back downstairs.

"I think the type of tree matters," I carefully explained. "This one is greener while the one downstairs is a mix of blue and green. This one has a conical shape to it and is bushier in appearance. The one downstairs is more pyramidal in shape."

Vance looked over at lawyer.

"Okay, I'll bite. What can you tell me about the trees?"

"Only that the trees up here were an afterthought," Jason admitted. "The tree downstairs is our main tree."

"Do you know what kind it is?" I asked.

Jason shrugged. "I think I heard that the two trees up here are noble firs. As for the tree downstairs, I'm not certain. I know I have the receipt somewhere. I always tell my clients that when you pay that much for something, even if it's a home-delivered tree, then it's always best to keep the receipt."

Vance and I shared a look. The tree downstairs was expensive? And it had been delivered?

"I'd very much like to see the receipt," Vance told the home owner, trying very hard to keep the excitement out of his voice.

"Sure thing," Jason nodded. "Let me see if I can find it. Would you care to come back downstairs?"

Vance and I both looked down at the corgis. Neither one of them gave the slightest sign of being interested in anything on the second floor. Sherlock wanted to go back downstairs and Watson wanted to do whatever her pack mate wanted.

"Sure thing. Vance? Grab Sherlock, would you?"

Ten minutes later Jason handed us the receipt for his tree. It was essentially a hand-written note detailing his purchase, namely that of a nine-foot Fraser fir, to be delivered to this address. The only mention of the seller was a scrawled Sticky Pines Delivery.

Vance and I both pulled out our phones. I was doing an Internet search while Vance began punching in numbers. He hit the hands-free option and we all listened to the phone line ring.

"Did you happen to get a number for this guy?" Vance asked.

Jason shook his head. "No. Sorry."

"Thank you for calling the Pomme Valley Police Department, this is Julie. How may I help you today?"

Harry's wife was one of the PVPD dispatchers.

"Hi, Julie, it's Vance. I need you to pull a permit for a

Christmas tree vendor who goes by Sticky Pines Delivery. And find out if any of our other vics had their trees delivered by this same company, okay?"

"I'm on it, Vance."

I nudged Vance.

"I found out about Fraser firs."

"What about them?" Vance asked disinterestedly.

"They're not native to this area," I told him. I directed my attention to Jason since he at least appeared interested in what I had to say. "Noble firs are. They're grown in the Pacific Northwest. Fraser firs are only grown in Virginia, North Carolina, and Tennessee. Vance, I think this is our common link. What do you want to bet that all the other burglaries had a Fraser fir in their house? That's why Sherlock didn't care about the tree I bought. I didn't pay that much for it, so it couldn't have been a Fraser fir."

"Where did you purchase this tree?" Vance asked, becoming more interested by the second. "Where were you specifically? Did he approach you or did you find him?"

"He was just a guy selling trees in a parking lot," Jason recalled. "I remember thinking that this was the way I used to pick out Christmas trees when I was a kid. So instead of going to the hardware store like I usually do, I stopped off and bought the tree from him."

"Where can we find his lot?" Vance asked as he pulled out his notebook.

"It's in the parking lot at Gary's Grocery."

"What about the delivery vehicle?" I asked. "Did you notice what he was driving?"

The lawyer nodded. "Sure. It was a white van. Why do you ask?"

TEN

O kay, you have made a believer out of me."

It was Tuesday, just after 11 a.m. I had given my parents a tour of Lentari Cellars, presented them with several bottles of the winery's finest, and had just started showing them around town. We passed Marauder's Grill when the scents hit my father and he looked just like Sherlock did whenever he smelled something he thought was appetizing. My father's nose lifted, I heard him sniff, and he started looking around.

"I thought you weren't keen on barbecue?" I remembered telling him.

"Whatever that was smelled fantastic."

Figuring it was close enough to lunchtime, I executed a flawless U-turn and headed back to the ramshackle shed that constituted my new favorite restaurant. I called Jillian to see if she was interested in meeting us for lunch—which she was—and she arrived a few minutes after we did.

My father took one look at where we were headed and was understandably hesitant. I ended up holding the door open a few minutes longer than necessary, since my parents were both a little skeptical of my choice of places for lunch. However, as soon as dad took his first bite of brisket, I knew he was hooked.

I looked at my father just before I sank my teeth into a rib slathered in barbecue sauce. Why is it conversation only seems to flow whenever you're unable to respond? It's inevitable. Take a huge bite of food at a restaurant and I guarantee you someone will walk by your table and ask how everything tastes.

"It's great, isn't it?" I added, once my mouth was clear. "If it wasn't for Jillian here, then I would never have stepped foot inside. It has quickly become my new favorite restaurant."

"There isn't much room in here," my mother commented, as she took another bite from her pulled pork sandwich. I knew from first-hand experience it was mouth-wateringly fantastic. But, she threw a wrench in the works when she ordered sweet potato fries instead of the regular variety. Blech.

My mother ate another fry and noticed my disapproving look. She reached for her basket, smiled at Jillian, and held a fry up with a questioning look on her face.

"Jillian, dear, you like sweet potatoes, don't you?"

Jillian nodded. "Of course, Mrs. Anderson. Whether they're covered in marshmallows or eaten like a baked potato, you can't go wrong with a sweet potato."

My mother shot me a victorious look.

"It's official, Zachary. You're the only one at the table who doesn't like sweet potatoes."

"Is that going to be a problem?" I asked.

Jillian laid her hand over mine.

"Of course not. Did you know, Mrs. Anderson, that I almost didn't get him through the door? He's very reluctant to try new things."

My mother smiled. "Oh, honey. What you see is just the tip of the iceberg. William and I raised that boy. We both know full well how stubborn he can be."

My eyes narrowed. My mother's mood had improved, but that was only because she had moved on to one of her favorite subjects to talk about: embarrassing stories about me. I looked over at Jillian and sighed.

"I'm not stubborn," I said. I wasn't being accused of anything, but I felt like I was obligated to say it. "I'm being choosy."

"You mean picky, right?" my father corrected.

Jillian giggled.

"Did you know that Zack once refused to touch a donut?" my mother asked conspiratorially.

Jillian turned to me with surprise all over her face.

"Really? Zack, lover of donuts, once didn't want to touch them?"

"They had to be a very specific kind of donut or else he'd turn up his nose at them," my mother recalled. "Crumb, if memory serves."

I groaned. If I had a nickel for every time I had heard this particular story, then I'd be a very rich man. I smiled at my mother. I couldn't get angry with her, not when she and Jillian seemed to be getting along.

"So when will you be picking up the dogs?" my father asked. "Are we headed back to the winery now?"

Surprised, I turned to my dad and grinned at him.

"I thought you always told me that dogs were just slobbery animals that you didn't want anything to do with."

Dad shrugged. "Your little Watson is certainly making me rethink my stance on dogs. I don't think I've ever seen such a sweet, gentle dog in my life."

"Did you hear that, Mom? I think Dad wants a dog."

"Oh, I don't know about that," my father said. He drank some of his iced tea and leaned back in his chair. "However, I do believe that if I had to then I would most certainly get a corgi."

Out of the corner of my eye I saw my mother beckon to Jillian. The two of them leaned close together. One whispered something to the other, which resulted in both of them laughing out loud.

I felt a tap on my shoulder.

"I'm proud of you, son," my father quietly said to me.

"Where is this coming from?" I asked, dropping my voice to match his.

"I'm sure you're wondering what we're doing here so early," my father softly added.

Both of us were keeping an eye on my mother. The last thing either of us needed was to be caught talking about her behind her back. I heard another round of giggling coming from the two of them and decided to leave them be.

"Yes, Dad, I am wondering. Why even come up here for Christmas? I know you don't like to travel for the holidays, especially for Christmas. And to top matters off, you and Mom showed up nearly a week early. What's going on? Are you guys spying on me?"

Surprisingly, my father nodded.

"There's no sense in beating around the bush about this. Look, son. It's been hard on your mother with you so far away. I know she's tried—unsuccessfully—to woo you back to Phoenix."

I felt myself growing angry.

"Dad, that isn't going to happen. My life is here in Pomme Valley now. I can't go back to Phoenix. I just can't."

"And that's what I kept telling your mother," Dad quietly explained. "There are too many painful memories for you waiting in Phoenix. I wouldn't want to revisit them anytime soon, either."

"Thanks for understanding," I gently told my father.

"You found a real winner there with your Jillian," my father continued. "Both your mom and I really like her."

"I'm not sure how to respond to that," I truthfully told my father. "Thanks? It's strange, dad. I feel … I feel…"

"Like you're cheating on Samantha?" my father quietly asked.

I nodded. "Yes. That's it. Exactly. A part of me feels like I'm being unfaithful to Sam and it makes me sick to my stomach."

"Samantha is gone, son. I'm sorry to say this, but there's nothing you can do to bring her back. Do you really think Samantha would want to see you like this? You need to move on, son. That's why I—we—are so proud of you. This is the first step we've seen you take that signifies you're finally looking to move on with your life."

"No," I corrected, "my first step was to move out here. I knew I couldn't call Phoenix home any more. It just hurt too much."

"Jillian is a lovely woman," my father said. "She's a good match for you."

"Thanks, Dad. That means a lot."

"So … are you able to tell me why you're working with the police?"

I gazed at my father and debated about how much I should tell him.

"Vance is a friend of mine. As I mentioned yesterday, he's a detective for the PVPD. He and I met under less than desirable circumstances."

"What's that supposed to mean?" my father curiously asked.

I heard Jillian's words in my head, asking if I really didn't get along with my parents. A sudden stab of guilt had me deciding to come clean. I took a deep breath.

"This isn't for Mom's ears," I said, dropping my voice even lower.

Intrigued, my father leaned close. We both checked on the girls. They were both chatting away, as though they had suddenly become the best of friends.

"I understand," Dad said. "What happened?"

"I was arrested for murder."

My father's eyebrows shot up.

"What? When?"

"Within twenty-four hours of moving here. Trust me, at the time I was thinking I had made the biggest mistake of my life moving here. This was also less than two hours after an old friend of mine from high school tricked me into adopting a dog."

"Watson," Dad guessed.

"Sherlock," I corrected. "Harry is the vet here in town. Little did I know that his veterinary office doubles as the local animal shelter. Anyway, the day before I moved to town, Pomme Valley had its first murder in fifty years."

"Why would they think you did it?" Dad asked.

The waitress came by and refilled our drinks.

"Because the person who was responsible left enough incriminating evidence to point the police my way."

"Son, I had no idea. Why didn't you call us for help? We could have helped. You know, we have an attorney on retainer!"

"I know you do," I said. "However, I didn't want to bother either of you. It was my decision to move here. It was my problem. I wanted to deal with it myself. Luckily, one of my readers is a lawyer. She's the one who got them to release me. Again, long story short, Sherlock is the one that kept finding the clues that helped prove my innocence. That little dog kept my butt out of jail."

"You're telling me Sherlock was able to find clues? What, like Scooby Doo?"

I grinned. "Kinda."

"Don't you think it was just luck?" Dad asked.

"Two months ago, in October, Sherlock helped crack the case of the fake mummy."

My dad almost choked on his iced tea.

"Would you care to run that by me again?"

"Let's just say that I had a very interesting Halloween, Dad."

"Sounds like it. And Sherlock was able to help solve the case?"

I nodded. "Yep. Sherlock pointed us in the right direction and even found the missing pendant."

My dad whistled with amazement. Both Jillian and my mother looked over. My dad and I grinned, waved, and went back to our conversation the moment they did, too.

"So that's why your detective friend wants your help."

"That's why my detective friend wants Sherlock's help," I corrected.

"Sherlock and Watson. Solving crimes again. How appropriate! And I do see why you don't want to tell your mother. I appreciate you telling me, though."

"I thought one of you ought to know, and of the two of you, you'd be able to handle the news better. I'll tell Mom if you think she needs to know."

"Let's give it some time and wait until she's not so emotional," my father suggested.

My cell phone rang. Sure enough, it was Vance. I showed the display to my dad. My mom and Jillian looked over at me. My mom might not have known who the Grinch's ring tone belonged to, but Jillian did.

"Hey Vance, what's up?"

"We've got an ID on the Grinch, buddy!"

"Oh, yeah? That's great! Who is it?" I muted my cell and relayed the news to the others.

"That's wonderful!" Jillian whispered.

"His name is Bob Geisel."

I frowned. Bob Geisel? Geisel? Wasn't that the real name of Dr. Seuss?

"Bob Geisel?" I slowly repeated. "Are you sure that his last name?"

"Yeah, I know. I triple-checked the name. I kinda feel like it must be an alias. All this talk of our Grinch and our suspect just happens to be named Geisel? Talk about the world's biggest coincidence."

"So what can you tell me about this guy?" I asked. "How'd you find him?"

"Let's see. Bob Geisel is a wanted felon in at least five states. I'm sure that number will be growing as we hear back from more agencies. He's wanted for felony breaking and entering, grand theft auto, and a few instances of aggravated assault."

"Well, now we can add murder to his list of accomplishments," I added.

"You've got that right."

"Why hasn't this guy been caught?" I asked. "How has he avoided the police when they know so much about him?"

"Because apparently he's a master of disguise. This guy knows how to disappear into the crowds by blending in. There's one report from Manassas, Virginia, which states that the reporting officer believed Geisel was a master of quick change."

"Quick change?" I repeated. "Is that where he can change his appearance in, like, ten seconds or less?"

"Yes. Looks like he's done just that on more than one occasion. Cops in Nashville had him under surveillance and were ready to bust him when he vanished right in front of their noses. Same story in Atlanta."

"So he's wanted for other burglaries," I said. "Do any of the reports say what he stole in the other cities?"

"I'm glad you asked. Presents, amigo. He always steals presents. Raleigh cops were the first ones credited with giving him the Grinch moniker."

"We're not the only ones referring to him as the Grinch, huh?" I asked. "What does he do with the presents? Does it say?"

I heard the rustling of paper as Vance started flipping through the reports he must have been holding.

"Most of the time they never resurface. There's only been one instance where one of the gifts had been found, and that's because it had been pawned. It was a Rolex. This would have been back in Virginia. Looks like Virginia Beach. Anyway, the Rolex was wrapped and sitting under the tree. Geisel obviously took it and pawned it, but he did so in Raleigh. It leads us to believe that he'll pawn the presents, but not until he makes it to another state."

"So there's hope these people can get their presents back," I said.

"If we can catch him before he leaves town, yes."

"Do you think he's still here?" I asked.

"Let's put it this way. We have put out an APB. Every single cop in this city is presently out on patrol, looking for this white van. Thus far we have bupkis."

"Want me to help look for it?" I asked. "The more eyes the merrier, right?"

"I don't think it matters right now, Zack. I think Geisel has fled. If he's been doing this as long as the reports say, then that means he's gotta know that we're on to him. I'd even go so far as to say he might have a police scanner."

"So you don't want our help?" I asked again, adding emphasis to 'our'.

A few seconds of silence passed.

"Ah. Tell you what. I wouldn't be disappointed if you and the dogs would like to go on a drive. But there is a stipulation, and it's a big one."

"I'm listening."

"If you find anything, and I do mean anything, then you phone it in. Is that understood?"

"You got it. Good luck. I'll keep you posted."

I hung up and looked at Jillian.

"Do you have to go back to work or would you like to go on a ride?"

"What's going on?" Jillian asked.

"I was going to go for a drive around the city. Maybe take the dogs. Let them get some fresh air."

"That sounds like a wonderful idea!" my mother exclaimed.

I cast a worried look at my dad. My father winked at me.

"You know what, Dana?" my dad said, rising to his feet. "Why don't we go have a latté over at Jillian's store? You mentioned to me last night that you wanted to look through her selection of cookbooks."

My mother frowned, "But I thought we could..."

This wasn't going as planned. I cast an imploring look at Jillian. Coming to my aid, she rose to her feet.

"Do you like to bake, Mrs. Anderson?"

My mother smiled. "Why yes, I do. My pies used to win awards. Do you bake?"

"Whenever I can. In fact, have you ever tried lingonberry pie? It's a Swedish dessert. One of my regulars is Swedish and has commented to me on more than one occasion that she used to enjoy a slice of lingonberry pie for Christmas. It reminded her of her grandmother. So, I made her one. It's up in the café."

"Lingonberry?" my mother repeated. Her brow furrowed. "I think I've heard of the berry, but I do not believe I have ever tried it."

My father ushered the two of them to the door.

"In that case, the first slice is on me. Son, catch up to us when you can."

"I will, Dad. I just have to wait for the check."

My father turned to look at me as he walked out the door.

"Already took care of it, son. See you soon!"

I put my wallet away. My dad and I have had a years-long competition to see who would be the one to pay for dinner. I used to snatch the check the moment it was deposited on the table. Man, did that make my dad mad. So he did everything he could to get the check handed to him. Making eye contact with the waiter, or else pulling them aside to give instructions. I have no idea what he did this time. It was the first time he had ever stepped foot inside.

Some things will never change.

I hurried home to get the dogs. Once we were headed back into town, I looked at Sherlock in the rear view mirror.

"You're up, pal. We need to find the Grinch. There's a good chance he's no longer in town, but just in case he happens to still be in PV, we need to be on the lookout for him."

Sherlock panted contentedly. The tri-color corgi stepped up onto the armrest of the window. I heard the telltale 'click' of the window opener. Just to humor him, I unlocked the windows. Sherlock's window promptly rolled down.

"Don't get used to this. This is only because we're helping Vance look for a van. You found one of them before, Sherlock. Let's see if you can find another one, okay?"

We drove around town for close to an hour. Up and down the side streets, like A through E, and even the numbered streets, including 1st through 5th. I didn't figure Geisel, if he was still in town, would be hiding anywhere near downtown. Maybe I had watched too many movies, but I thought that if Geisel was hiding, then it'd be on a small, less traveled side street.

No luck.

For kicks and giggles, I turned my Jeep onto Main. I slowly cruised past all the shops, stores, and restaurants. There was no way this guy could be hiding in broad daylight. I don't care how good of a disguise he was wearing, he'd never risk it. No one was that ballsy.

I kept an eye on Sherlock. He had grown bored of the drive and had curled up on the back seat. I could tell he wasn't sleeping, but if something didn't happen soon then I was expecting to hear his snores within the next several minutes.

I was approaching Oregon Street and turned right, now heading north. Just then Sherlock's head lifted. He was at the window in a flash. I checked the mirror to make sure no one was behind me and slowed to a crawl. Sherlock sniffed the air a few times before letting out an audible snort. He returned to the seat.

Curious, I waited for the traffic to clear and executed another U-turn. Now we were heading south on Oregon, approaching Main. As I came to a stop at an intersection Sherlock perked up again. Once the lights turned green, and I headed through the intersection, Sherlock returned to his seat.

One more U-turn later and we were back at the same intersection. Yep, Sherlock had his head back through the window, sniffing the air. Since I had a few moments to kill while waiting for the light, I looked around. The only thing at this particular intersection was Apple Valley Rentals, the one and only outdoor shop catering to those who wanted to rent scooters, ATVs, kayaks, and so on.

Puzzled, I looked at Sherlock. Why would he be interested in a rental shop? But, just for the heck of it, I pulled off and decided to circle the store with my Jeep.

Keeping an eye on the dogs, I started circling the building. Thankfully the business had a lot of parking, and I could make a complete circuit of the store. Sherlock, on the other hand, hadn't paid any attention to the store whatsoever. As I was driving around the back side, however, he perked up again and woofed a warning. I brought the Jeep to a stop, put it in park, and turned to look at him.

He was looking west, past Apple Valley Rentals. What was back there? Rupert's Gas & Auto. It was Pomme Valley's busiest gas station.

We headed toward the gas station when I noticed Sherlock wasn't looking at the station, per se, but at the large open stalls on the right. They were stalls where you could wash your own car at your own expense by feeding quarters into the machinery.

More curious than anything, I pulled up in front of the two stalls and parked. Sherlock had started barking. Watson had joined him at the window and was barking, too, only I knew the only reason she was barking was because of Sherlock.

I scanned the area first, making sure there weren't any vans. I needed to find out what had attracted Sherlock's attention and to verify it was legit before I called Vance. I know he wanted me to inform him should Sherlock express interest in anything, but I wanted confirmation first.

Deciding it was safe, I put their royal highnesses down on the ground. Sherlock guided me to the stall on the right. I gave the corgi a quizzical look.

"Ok, we're here. What about it?"

Sherlock walked over to the drain and sniffed at it. Curious, I looked down at the grating. I didn't see anything, although there was some sort of milky residue visible inside the drain.

Then it hit me like a ton of bricks. It was paint! Geisel must have had water-soluble paint on his van. We were looking for a white van when it was now a different color!

Hmm, this guy was good.

I whipped out my cell, took a picture of the drain, and sent it to Vance with the following caption:

Sherlock had me stop at the car wash stalls next to Rupert's Gas. Found this inside the drain. We're not looking for a white van anymore.

Five seconds. That's how long it took for Vance to call.

"He changed the color of his van. He knew we'd be on to him! That jerk is smart!"

"That means the van we're looking for could be any color. Do you have any idea how many vans are in Pomme Valley?"

"No, but give me a few seconds and I can. Hold on."

I heard my friend shuffle around a bit. He must have held a hand over the phone because I heard bits of a muffled conversation. It sounded like he was relaying the news about the van's color change to someone else.

"Are you there?"

"Yeah."

"I let the captain know. He's pissed. He wants this guy found. It feels like Geisel has duped the whole town. Captain Nelson wants to be the one to, and I quote, wipe that smug smile off of Geisel's face, end quote."

I heard a whine and automatically looked down. Watson had spotted some kids playing nearby. They looked to be ten or eleven. Three boys and two girls. Leave it to Watson to want to play.

Kids playing.

I figured the kids had been released for Christmas break. How long had they been playing there? Could one of them have seen the van and might possibly know what color it had become?

"Zack? Did you hear me? There are 102 vans registered in PV. Unless we know a few more details then we have nothing to go on."

"I may have something," I told Vance as I walked toward the kids. "Hold on. I'm going to put the phone in my pocket. Keep listening."

"What are you...?"

I didn't hear the rest. I approached the kids and smiled at them. The girls saw the two dogs and immediately oohed and aahed over them. Both Sherlock and Watson wiggled with anticipation.

"Hi there!" I said. "I was wondering if one of you could help me out."

The kids were silent as they studied me. Then, with a start, I had to laugh. At the moment, I was exactly what all parents warn their children about. A stranger with dogs.

"We're not supposed to talk to strangers," a blond girl with her hair in a long braid, primly informed me.

I nodded. "You're absolutely right. You're not. I was just wondering if any of you happened to see a white van go into one of those car wash stalls and then come out a different color."

One of the boys nodded. "I saw one do that."

"How long ago?" I excitedly asked.

"Why do you want to know?" the same girl asked.

I read somewhere that most kids appreciated being treated like adults and didn't care for anyone who spoke down to them. I decided to be upfront and honest.

"Have you heard about the Grinch who is stealing presents from under people's Christmas trees?" I asked.

All five of the kids nodded.

"Well, that's him. He drives a white van. Now, in an effort to get away before the police can get him, he washed off the white paint on his van. Now, it'd be incredibly helpful if someone could tell me what color it was when it left that stall."

"It was dark," the other girl, a brunette, said. "It was hard to see. We were way over there when he pulled away."

The girl pointed to a section of open grass between the rental store and the gas station.

"Did anyone else get a good look at the van?" I continued. "Any idea what color it was? Did it have anything written on the side of it? Darkened windows?"

"I think it was blue," one of the boys decided. "Dark blue. I don't remember seeing any tinted windows."

"You're right," the third boy agreed. "No tinted windows. My brother's car has tinted windows. This one didn't."

"And the color?" I pressed.

"Dark blue," the first boy said.

"Black," the second boy disagreed.

"Dark gray?" the third boy offered.

"Does anyone have any idea how long ago he washed his van?" I asked.

"About an hour ago," the blond girl answered. "I know

'cause I had just received a text from my mom, wanting to know where we were."

I smiled at the kids. "Thanks, guys. That's been incredibly helpful. Have fun, okay?"

"Will do, mister," one boy replied.

The kids moved off as I pulled the cell out of my pocket.

"Did you get all that?"

"Every word. Nice job, Zack. I've already sent out word that we're looking for a dark van. At this point, each and every van that fits the bill will be pulled over and checked out."

"Good to hear. I want those presents to be returned to their families."

"All I want for Christmas is to catch this culprit."

"If he's still in town, then we'll get him, pal."

"I'll hold you to it, Zack."

I decided to head back down Main. I had a hunch that somehow not only was this guy still in PV, he was hiding right out in the open. This smug nitwit had figured he had given us the slip by changing the color of his van. He was out there. Somewhere.

The cruise down Main was uneventful. Sherlock and Watson enjoyed sticking their snouts out the windows, don't get me wrong. But neither of them showed any interest in anything besides the occasional woof at another dog. We were approaching Gary's Grocery on the east side of town when, on a whim, I decided to pull in to check out the area where Geisel had set up shop selling trees.

I glanced over at the destruction of the Square L store. One over-sized bulldozer had made short work of the building. A loader was now scooping up debris to dump it in one of the two dump trucks idling nearby.

A horn blasted me back to reality. While gazing at the destroyed store I had inadvertently drifted off course and threatened the oncoming traffic. I hastily flipped on the signal and prepared to cut into the grocery store's parking lot. The driver of the UPS van I almost hit gestured angrily at me before turning west, onto Main.

"That could've been bad," I grumbled to myself, at the exact same time Sherlock lost his mind.

Sherlock reared up onto his hind legs so that he could look out the window. His barks were so fierce that you'd think he had caught sight of the boogeyman himself. I swear I saw Watson shrug her shoulders and then start barking, too.

"What is wrong with you?" I asked, raising my voice to be heard over his barks. "There's nothing out there but the…"

The van! I had almost hit a UPS van! It was a dark brown. That certainly could have been the van the kids had seen!

I hurriedly dialed Vance.

"Hey Zack, what's going…"

"Vance! I think I saw him!"

"What?! Where?"

"He's in a brown UPS van. He was just leaving the parking lot at the grocery store when I almost hit him."

"When you what?"

"I'll explain later. He turned onto Main, heading south!"

"I'm on it! Good work, Zack!"

"It wasn't me; it was Sherlock. He went crazy as soon as we passed that van. I didn't even give the van a second look. It's Christmastime. You'd expect to see delivery vans out and about."

"It's Geisel, Zack. I just know it! I gotta go!"

"Go get him, buddy!"

I decided to head back down Main, heading west. I wanted to see if I could perhaps follow the van, in case it tried to duck into an alley somewhere in order to lose any possible tails. However, as I merged onto Main, I saw that wasn't going to be a problem.

The van had made it about three blocks when cop cars had swooped in from all directions. Guns had been drawn and the driver was now being held at gunpoint. I watched Vance's sedan turn off of Oregon and tear down Main, heading toward us, with a single cherry light placed directly over the driver's side of the car. I had to laugh. I hadn't seen one of those on a car since the '80s.

"What's going on?" I heard the driver demand. "What's wrong with you people? You have no reason to pull me over! Are you trying to get me fired?"

"What's your name?" Vance asked, as soon as he exited his vehicle.

"Rick Burton. Why?"

I watched Vance slowly walk around the van. As he approached the rear driver side wheel well, I saw him stoop, run his fingers along the inside of the well, and then straighten. His fingers had a white smudge on them.

"Well, Mr. Burton, I ... or should I call you Mr. Geisel? We've been looking for you. You're under arrest for murder, and for..."

The driver took off like a shot. However, the PVPD were waiting. The closest police officer already had his Taser ready. He calmly raised his weapon, drew a bead on his target, and fired a single shot as Geisel ran by. In less than five seconds it was over. The police pulled Geisel, who was still twitching uncontrollably, to his feet and placed him under arrest.

Vance looked through the back windows of the van and pulled both doors wide open. We all looked in. There was a huge tarp covering something in the cargo area of the van. Vance pulled the tarp off and whistled with amazement.

A small mountain of presents met our eyes.

ELEVEN

"Why is everyone staring at me?" I asked as I stared at my eerily quiet living room.

To best explain this, I need you to let me backtrack just a bit.

It was Christmas day and things were hopping at the Anderson house. Jillian, Hannah, and my mom were in the kitchen prepping snack trays and setting out dishes. They were laughing, chatting, and sometimes going so quiet I had to wonder what they were all talking about. I could only hope my name stayed out of it. I tried several times to wander into the kitchen to see about offering some type of help but, as I was quick to learn, my kitchen wasn't designed for four. Aunt Bonnie's house may not have been tiny, but by no means could it be considered a manor. I would have been underfoot, and two of the three women were presently armed with knives. I think I'll wait in the living room, thank you very much.

Speaking of guests, I was also expecting Vance a little later on, along with his family. He and Tori had agreed to have dinner with us provided they can host next year. It was a deal I was more than happy to make. If Vance, Tori, and their two girls do happen to show, and I see no reason why they wouldn't show, then that would put the occupancy rate at ten. I don't think I've ever had that many people over at my house before in my life. Well, unless you count the time when a dead dude appeared in my winery just up the hill, but that was another story.

Once the trays of snacks had been laid out, and everyone helped themselves to a plate of food, we all sat down to contemplate the mountain of presents that was under the tree. I glanced over at Sherlock and Watson. Both were by the fireplace enjoying the warmth of the fire. Watson was on her back and Sherlock was stretched out next to her. Both were content to watch the activity in the room, although Watson was watching it from an upside down angle. However, that came to a screeching halt the moment Colin bit into a carrot. Both corgis were on their feet in a flash and had presented themselves before the boy, hoping a little morsel of orange goodness might find its way to the floor.

"Do they eat carrots?" Colin asked, giving me a skeptical look.

"Yep," I confirmed. "They each love them. I don't give them too much. Bite off tiny little pieces and let them have that."

Colin nodded. He bit a baby carrot into a few pieces

and gingerly handed each to the dogs. Both dogs took the proffered carrots as gently as they could.

"Brown-nosers," I muttered, eliciting a laugh from my father.

Presents were passed around. Within moments, everyone had a small stack of gifts, waiting to be opened. I picked up the closest present with my name on the tag and hesitated. The entire room had gone eerily quiet. I looked up and was surprised to see every single person staring at me as though I had just let one rip. And I hadn't.

There, see? Now we're caught up.

"Seriously, guys. Feel free to dig in."

"But this way everyone gets to see what you were given," Jillian argued.

"Look at how many presents there are," I reminded her. "If we do this only one at a time then poor Colin there will have graduated high school before we're done."

I heard Colin snicker.

Jillian looked at my parents.

"Well, what do you think, Dana?"

Certain I had won this particular argument; my hand was poised to rip the paper clean off the gift sitting in my lap. I groaned and looked over at my mom. She was watching me with a smile on her face.

"I think we can probably all open a present, but as soon as each gift is revealed, then I think that person should announce what they were given and thank the giver."

Jillian nodded. "I like that. That seems fair."

"That seems pointless," I muttered. Jillian swatted me on the arm.

The ripping of paper commenced. Bows, ribbon, and wadded paper went flying everywhere. I had the foresight to bring in a large trash can, so thankfully most of the discarded wrappings went into the waste can. My father and I soon began a contest to see who could land the most shots in the can, all without either of us breaking our seated positions.

"What do you have there, Colin?" I asked as I watched the boy unwrap a present I had personally wrapped myself.

"I'm not sure," Colin admitted. "It's heavy, whatever it is."

"If it's heavy, then it's expensive," Hannah told her son. "Be careful with it."

Colin ripped the first strip of paper from the package and froze. His eyes widened with surprise. He quickly finished unwrapping the gift and nudged his mother's shoulder.

"What is…? Colin, is that what I think it is?"

Colin held the brand new microscope aloft. Now, don't get the wrong idea. I'm not trying to spoil the boy. Microscopes come in all shapes and sizes. I didn't buy him one of the super fancy ones, but more of a nicer "amateur" scope. I had a similar one when I was a kid and I loved it. Hannah had mentioned a few times that her son absolutely loves math and science. I saw a little of myself in the boy so I thought I'd get him something that I knew he'd really enjoy.

"Who's it from?" Hannah asked.

Colin's eyes dropped to the shreds of paper lying at his feet.

"Umm, I'm not sure?"

"You mean you opened that gift without checking to see who it was from? You'd better find that tag, young man."

Colin began inspecting the remnants of his microscope's wrapping. He finally found the piece with what was left of the tag. He showed it to his mother.

"It says, 'To Colin from Santa.' That's it."

"Give me that," Hannah demanded.

She inspected the tag and narrowed her eyes. I knew exactly what she was doing. She was trying to identify 'Santa' by the writing. Well, good luck. The only writing of mine she was familiar with was the Victorian cursive style of handwriting I used whenever I was signing books as my alter ego. This time I signed that tag using my own natural handwriting.

"Who gave him this?" Hannah asked the room. "One of you must have done it."

"Didn't the tag say it was from Santa?" Jillian innocently asked.

Hannah quickly pulled the torn strip of paper up before her eyes. My guess is that she was trying to see if it could've been written by Jillian. It wasn't. I've seen Jillian write before. Her penmanship could easily be mistaken for calligraphy. It most certainly wasn't her.

"Well, I'd like to speak to Santa to thank him personally for this."

"Well, the next time I see him I'll let him know you're looking for him," Jillian quipped, eliciting a frown from Hannah.

"Who's next?" my mother asked the room. "Hannah, what do you have there?"

Colin pulled the torn strip of wrapping paper from her hands and tossed it into the trash. He picked up the present sitting next to his mother on the couch and placed it into her hands.

"Here, Mom. Open this."

"This is from you, isn't it?" Hannah asked as she caught sight of the tag.

"Yep. Go ahead. Open it."

Hannah opened her small cardboard box to reveal ... a DVD case. On it was a customized label that had a picture of Colin and his mother, both smiling for the camera. Hannah slowly opened the case and looked at the DVD.

"Do you remember," Colin started explaining, "how you were telling me that you had all these videos that you wanted to burn onto a DVD so that we could watch them on the TV? Well, there you go."

"How did you do this?" Hannah asked with a shocked expression on her face. "I've been trying to figure out how to do this all summer!"

"All it takes is someone who's done it before," I quietly quipped. "And the right computer setup."

Hannah clutched the video to her chest and mouthed thank you to me when Colin looked away. I nodded. It had been an easy request to fulfill. Colin had actually approached me to see if I knew how to do it.

I watched Jillian pick up the small package that I knew was from me. She caught sight of the name on the tag and looked over at me. I grinned, gave her hand a squeeze, and encouraged her to open it.

"Let's see what we have here," Jillian murmured as she worked to remove the wrappings and ribbon I had used. The problem was, I remembered that I had probably used half a container of tape to make sure the paper stayed in place. "I don't think I've seen this much tape on one package before, Zachary."

I grinned. "Hey, better safe than sorry."

"What do you have there?" my mother asked.

"It's something small, almost like a..." Jillian gasped as the cover of the small box came off.

Inside the box was a simple gold pocket watch. It had large numerals depicting the hours and an additional dial near the bottom which depicted the seconds. The watch showed some signs of wear, but that wasn't surprising, since it was over seventy years old. This one, I knew, dated from 1941.

Hannah had told me, back in the coffee shop nearly two weeks ago, that Jillian had been looking for a very specific type of pocket watch for a long time now. Apparently, her grandfather had served in World War 2 and his squadron had all been given this model of pocket watch. Her grandfather had given this watch to her years ago, when she was a little girl, and as luck would have it, she had lost it.

She has regretted it ever since. Hannah told me that Jillian had been searching for a replacement, but hadn't had any luck since she didn't know which model of watch her grandfather's squadron had been given.

Well, behold the power of the internet. I had tracked down the squadron that her grandfather had belonged to, looked up the names of its members, and started making phone calls. I finally contacted a surviving member who was nice enough to send me a dozen or so pictures—with the help of his great-great-granddaughter—and after another hour or so, I had come up with the model.

It was an Elgin 657 Shockmaster pocket watch, with 17 jewels, only I didn't see any jewels on it. Whatever. It had a rolled 10k gold plate and an Elgin Star Dial sunk with 1-60 on the outer chapter ring.

I never knew watches could be so precise.

Armed with that information, I quickly found several people selling them on eBay. I found one that was working, paid for expedited shipping, and the rest was history.

"Is this ...?" Jillian began. Her voice broke.

My mother got up from her seat on the couch and moved closer so she could see what Jillian was holding.

"What do you have there, Jillian?" my father curiously asked.

Jillian reverently picked the watch up and held it by its chain so that we could all see it.

"This is the same model watch that my grandfather gave me when I was a little girl that I had lost. I've been looking to find a replacement for years. Zachary Anderson, how did you find it?"

I grinned at Hannah before looking Jillian's way.

"Well, let's just say that I'm good on a computer."

"This means the world to me. Thank you."

"You're welcome."

"Open mine now," Jillian instructed.

I found Jillian's delicately wrapped present and studied it. It was about the size of a normal hardcover book, only this package wasn't heavy like a book. What could it be? I gave the present an obligatory shake—no sound—and tore off the wrapping. I stared, dumbfounded, at the item nestled within.

Okay, in order to explain this, I have to put on my Nerd Hat. We nerds like to collect things. Action figures, swords, collectibles, and anything that most normal people would roll their eyes at would typically find their way to a shelf or a closet somewhere in a nerd's house. As for me, I had a room upstairs that was dedicated to my collectibles. My main passions are collecting swords—crazy, I know—and collecting all things Star Wars. One of the most sought-after items I had been looking for was a Luke Skywalker figurine with what was referred to as a double-telescoping light saber. The 'double-telescoping' just referred to the early mechanics used to give Luke's lightsaber some length. Three figures were released with the 'T stamp. Luke, Ben, and Darth Vader. I had Ben and Vader, but I still needed Luke.

Not anymore.

How Jillian found this, or even knew that I was looking for it, was beyond me. Trying to buy me something that I didn't already have in my Star Wars collection was akin to trying to find the one penny that a serious numismatist didn't already own. No one knew about Luke. No one, except for…

I glanced at my father. He had the biggest grin on his face that I have ever seen. My eyes narrowed. I looked over at Jillian. I then thought back to what she had said the moment she had first met my parents.

It is good to finally meet you…

So, that explained why Jillian hadn't been rattled when I told her that my parents were in town a week early. She had been in contact with them! Wow. I never saw that coming.

Jillian leaned close. "I hope you like it."

"I love it. You sneak. Thank you."

A quick thirty minutes later it looked like a tornado had hit the living room. Yes, most of the trash had made it into the trash can. However, I'm talking about two mischievous canines who thought it was great fun stealing wads of wrapping paper and playing tug with it. Then, of course, Sherlock's favorite game came next, which was keep away. I tasked Colin with making sure Sherlock stayed away from the trash.

Sherlock was up for the challenge. He and Watson kept Hannah's son chasing after them for close to twenty minutes. I'm not sure who pooped out first, the dogs or the boy. One minute they were running through the living room as though the devil himself was hot on their tails, and the next? Colin had collapsed on the couch and both dogs were out cold right next to him. It was such a cute picture that Hannah actually pulled out her cell and snapped a few pics.

"They've finally run out of energy," I quietly said.

Hannah smiled fondly at her son.

"I really should consider getting him a dog. It's just that I know Dylan hates dogs."

"That's too bad," I said. "Colin is very good with dogs. Look at him. He's gentle, he's firm, but he won't tolerate them getting too aggressive. He'd be perfect."

"I know," Hannah agreed. "Hopefully someday."

"Well, if it's okay with you, I'd like to add Colin to my list of dog sitters. I've used Woody's daughter a few times, but she's not always available."

Hannah visibly brightened. "Why yes! I'm sure he'd love that. Thank you, Zachary."

The doorbell rang. The dogs, who were snoozing up on the couch with Colin, who had just drifted off, started barking. In fact, I think they woke up without realizing what they should be barking at. Sherlock jumped down and continued to bark. He looked at me, at Jillian, and finally at my father as he tried to figure out who woke him up.

Jillian made it to the door first.

"Merry Christmas!" Vance announced as he and Tori came through the door. Two young girls I hadn't met before timidly followed them inside.

We were introduced to Tiffany, age nine, and Victoria, age eleven. They took up residence on the end of the couch, talking quietly with one another. I glanced over at Sherlock. He was watching the girls like a mother bear would watch her young.

"Awwooooo!"

Both girls looked up, saw Sherlock watching them, and began an animated discussion. I signaled Sherlock to wait and walked over to the girls. I noticed Vance was watching me, so I gave him a wink and looked at Sherlock. Vance glanced over, saw that Sherlock was eagerly waiting to be released, and then nudged Tori. Together they surreptitiously moved closer so they wouldn't miss the introduction.

"Would you girls like to meet the dogs?"

"Are they friendly?" Victoria asked. "Dad talks about the one called Sherlock all the time."

"Which one is he?" Tiffany asked.

I pointed at Sherlock.

"He's the one sitting closest to the fire. He's the one that has some black on him. Watson is there in front of the fire. She doesn't have any black anywhere. Do you two like dogs?"

Both girls nodded.

"Would you like to meet them?"

The girls nodded again.

"May I recommend that you both scoot back on the couch?"

Victoria gave me a puzzled look.

"Why?"

"It's so your back has some support when they come up to say hello."

Tiffany turned to look at the back of the couch. Being as small as they were, both of the girls were sitting on the end of the couch. They had about two feet of empty space directly behind them.

"We're okay," Victoria assured me.

I grinned. It was exactly what I wanted to hear. I looked over at their parents. Tori was holding her phone up, no doubt recording what was about to happen.

I walked over to Sherlock and laid my arm across his back. Watson had rolled onto her feet and was watching me, too. I looked back at the girls.

"Ready?"

The look I received from the older girl suggested she thought I was the stupidest thing on two legs. As you may recall, it wasn't the first time that particular thought had come up in the last week or so. I ruffled the fur behind Sherlock's ears.

"Okay, boy. Are you ready?"

Sherlock barked excitedly.

"All right. Here we go. And ... release!"

Sherlock bounded toward Victoria, who shrieked with surprise. The tri-color corgi cleared the distance from the ground to the couch in a single leap, knocking Victoria onto her back and covering her face with corgi kisses. Watson had also rushed over, but stopped just short of jumping up on Tiffany. She reared up on her hind legs and yipped excitedly. Tiffany smiled and patted Watson on her head.

An excited squeal came from Tiffany's left. Victoria was

on her back, arms flailing, as she tried to dodge Sherlock's tongue. The corgi, unfortunately for her, was much quicker. I casually stood, walked calmly over to the couch, and picked Sherlock up off the girl. I shifted Sherlock so that I was supporting his weight with my right arm and pulled Victoria back to an upright position with my left.

"Are you okay? I tried to warn you."

"Omigod! That dog ... that dog ... is so cute!"

"You've been officially inducted into his pack," I explained to Vance's oldest daughter. I glanced over at Tiffany, who was staring at Sherlock with wide, unblinking eyes. As if noticing her for the first time, Sherlock had now locked eyes on Tiffany and was whining to be let down.

"Aww! He wants to say hello to me, too!"

"Are you okay with that?"

Tiffany nodded. "I love dogs!"

I glanced over at Vance. He gave a nod of approval. Tori was still filming.

"Okay. Sherlock, meet young Tiffany!"

I set Sherlock on the ground and let go. Less than two seconds later Tiffany was experiencing her own invitation to join Sherlock's pack. She laughed hysterically while the corgi lunged forward to lick her cheeks, face, forehead, and anything else his long tongue could reach.

Afterwards, after we had all finished dinner and were trying to resist the urge to slip into food induced comas, Vance let out an exclamation of surprise. He clinked his wine glass a few times to make sure he had everyone's attention. I set down my glass of sparkling apple juice and waited to see what he had to say.

"Sorry guys, but I forgot to tell you. Remember the Grinch? Bob Geisel?"

"He's rather hard to forget," I chuckled.

"Well, he was arraigned today. In New York. Turns out that's where his spree of burglaries started. They were first to lay claim on our Grinch. Turns out he was born there."

"Was Geisel his real name?" I asked.

Vance nodded. "Yes. I've read the reports. The guy had a rough childhood. Been in and out of juvenile hall so many times that the state lost count. Busted for stealing, breaking and entering, and a list of other offenses so long that it'd take too long to read them all. He's been doing this for so long that he's a wanted man in fourteen different states, most of which are on the east coast. The only states that want him out west are us and Idaho."

I whistled with amazement.

"I wonder why he moved out west," Jillian said. "Maybe things became too difficult for him on the east coast?"

Vance shrugged. "Probably. The most recent report, before he headed west, came from Raleigh, North Carolina. That's the case where the locals were closing in on him and were only moments away from apprehending him when he up and disappeared right from under their noses."

"He quick-changed his appearance," I guessed.

"Right. He must've figured things were getting too hot and that the local cops were on to his methods so he headed as far away as he could without getting on a boat or a plane. He came to the Pacific Northwest."

"What a piece of work," I said. "I'm glad he's locked up. I hated to think that a guy like that could pretty much waltz right into any house he wanted and take whatever suited him."

"Speaking of which," Vance said as he snapped his fingers, "guess what was found in a hidden compartment of his van?"

"More presents?" I guessed.

Vance shook his head. "Nope. A ring of keys. Bumping keys. He could get past any tumbler lock in a matter of a few seconds, all without leaving any trace of his presence behind. It was spooky. Still is, if you ask me."

"Well, our new locks certainly help me sleep better at night," Tori added.

Jillian held up her glass and clinked it with Tori's, "Hear, hear."

"I heard from Jim the other day," Vance continued. "Our new locksmith has been so busy that he's hired two additional guys to help him out. Apparently, his business is booming."

"No arguments there," I said. "Once it became known how Geisel was getting in and out of the houses, then practically the whole town ordered new sets of locks. I don't blame them. That's the first thing we all did."

"Did those families get back their presents?" my mother asked.

Vance nodded. "For the most part. Geisel wasn't gentle on any of the packages. Some were damaged. Some had the tags torn off. We had the families come down to try and identify what was theirs."

"There's something I want to know," Harry said as he took Julie's hand. "How did the Murphy family manage to afford that fancy tree? Didn't you say they didn't have any extra money? I just can't see them going out of their way to spend that much dough on a tree. If money was that tight, then I sure would be spending it on my kids and not on some tree."

Julie patted his hand, "I know you would, babe."

Vance had just taken a large swallow of his drink when he snorted.

"Didn't I tell you? Could've swore I did."

"Tell us what?" Harry asked.

"Well, turns out the Murphy family had that tree 'cause the father won it at his company's office Christmas party. The owner of the company had bought one of Geisel's trees, liked it, and essentially bought another with the intent of giving it away at the company party. All the winner had to do was go down to the lot and claim the tree."

"And I suppose Geisel delivered the tree, like all the others?" Jillian asked.

Vance nodded. "Yep."

"I still don't understand why Geisel only stole the presents," Tori said. "What a horrible thing to do to a family just before Christmas."

Vance shrugged and held out his hands in surrender.

"We may never know. If I were to venture a guess, I'd say it was because of Geisel's difficult upbringing. Here was a kid who was first busted for breaking and entering before he was twelve. As far as anyone was concerned, he didn't have a home life. Thanks to his last name he probably hated Christmas. Maybe it annoyed him to see others enjoy Christmas when he didn't have any fond memories of it? Who can say?"

"That's no way to live," Jillian quietly said.

"I concur," Tori agreed.

"At least the families got their gifts back," Jillian said. "I'm excited the Murphy family will have a great Christmas this year."

"The father did his darndest to try and give the presents back," Vance recalled. "I had to tell him that the Secret Santa responsible wouldn't be pleased."

"You can bet your ass I wouldn't be," I grumbled.

"Zachary!" Jillian hissed. She pointed at Vance's

daughters. "Language!"

"It's okay," Victoria said as she smiled at me. "I've heard worse."

"You have?" Tori asked, frowning. "From who? When?"

Both girls pointed at their father. Vance blushed and smiled sheepishly. Tori frowned.

"I see that I need to have a chat with your father. We'll schedule that for another time."

Vance sighed. "Yes, dear."

"Zachary," my mother said, drawing my attention. "How are the sales of your new romance novel going?"

The table fell silent. I groaned and leaned forward to rest my head on the table. I heard Vance snicker.

"Romance novels? You write romance novels, pal?"

"You do?" Tori asked, surprised. "I love romance novels. I don't remember ever seeing your name on one before."

"Thanks, Mom."

By the time I leaned back in my chair I'm sure I was as red as a lobster.

"Zachary," my mother chided, "you haven't told your friends what types of books you write?"

"Obviously not, Mom."

My mother looked at me and then at my friends. A mischievous twinkle appeared in her eye. She looked at Vance and smiled.

"You won't find his name on any of his books because he uses a pseudonym."

"He uses a what?" Victoria asked, turning to her mother.

"He uses a different name when he writes," Tori answered. She fixed me with a direct stare. "What name do you use?"

Well, the cat was out of the bag. There was no point in hiding it anymore. And you know what? I was glad. I was tired of hiding what I do from my friends. I can only imagine my mother sensed this.

"The name I use is ... Hannah? Would you like to tell them?"

Jillian's head slowly swiveled until she was looking at her friend.

"You know what name he uses? How? When did you know?"

"I've had my suspicions for a while now," Hannah answered. She giggled. "It wasn't until a few weeks ago when I confronted Zachary with what I knew and he admitted I was right. Ladies and gentlemen, boys and girls, meet Chastity Wadsworth."

Tori spewed her drink, while Jillian choked on hers. I also heard Vance snickering at me. However, his laughter died off once he saw the look of astonishment on his wife's face.

"Wait, have you read his books?"

"Every one!" Tori exclaimed, bursting into giggles. "Oh, Zack, what an imagination you have! I love your books!"

"You're Chastity Wadsworth?" Jillian incredulously repeated. "I've read all your books, too. I even wrote you a fan letter."

"You did?" I asked, surprised.

"Yes. And you even wrote back. I still have it!"

"The two of you corresponded before," Hannah softly mused. "Simply incredible."

"To be fair, at the time I thought he was a woman."

Vance snickered again. Tiffany and Victoria giggled,

too. I shrugged.

"It's a living."

"Jillian," Hannah said, catching her friend's attention, "I think we need to show him."

"Show him what?" Jillian asked.

Hannah pointed back into the kitchen.

"Remember what we put in the laundry room?"

Jillian's face lit up. "I do! How could I have forgotten? Zachary, wait right here. Hannah? Would you help me?"

Hannah pushed away from the table, "Sure!"

"What's going on?" Vance asked.

I shrugged and held up my hands. "No clue."

"I'm very sorry I let your secret out, Zachary," my mother said.

"No you're not," I laughed. "You know what, Mom? It's okay. We're all friends here. I don't mind them knowing."

"There's something I need to tell you, Zachary," my mother began. "I'm aware your father told you that my intent for this visit was to persuade you to move back to Phoenix."

I nodded. "I know. I told dad that it wasn't going to happen. My life is here now."

My mom nodded. "I can see that. I wanted to tell you that I'm proud of you for taking the steps to return to a normal life after Samantha died."

"Who's Samantha?" Victoria asked.

"Shush, honey," Vance whispered.

"It's okay," I told Vance. I looked at his oldest daughter and smiled wistfully. "Samantha was my wife. She was killed in a car accident a little over a year ago."

Victoria's young face fell. She hung her head.

"I'm sorry."

"Look, young lady," I said, using a mock stern voice.

"If you don't start smiling again, then I'm going to sic Sherlock on you. I'm sure he'd love to give you corgi kisses again."

Victoria brightened and giggled. I smiled back at the girl. I glanced over at Vance, who nodded that everything was okay.

"This box sure is heavy," I heard Hannah say as both she and Jillian came back in carrying a box between them.

They set it on the kitchen counter after Tori and Vance cleared away some dishes.

"So what's in here?" I asked as I stepped away from the table.

"Something you need to see," Jillian told me. "I think it'll answer the question I've heard you ask several times."

"And that is?" I prompted.

"Why you and Samantha were given Lentari Cellars."

My eyes fixated on the box.

"Really? You're right. I've wanted to know the answer to that for a long time. Alrighty then. Open it up."

Vance pulled the box top up and off the base. Together we all looked into the box. I gasped with surprise. Inside were copies of my books. All of my books, from the looks of things. Aunt Bonnie had been a fan of mine! Why hadn't I seen this before?

I looked back at the top portion of the box. In Aunt Bonnie's neat scrawl were the words Christmas Decorations. Well, that explains why I had brought the box down from the attic.

"Look at this," Jillian exclaimed, pulling out several yellowing newspapers.

Once the papers were carefully unfolded, we saw that the papers contained articles and reviews about my books. I flipped through page after page from various newspapers. It looked as though any time a book of mine made headlines, or else was mentioned in a review, Aunt Bonnie had kept the paper.

"She was a fan of your romance books," Vance snorted, earning a harsh stare from Tori. "How's that make you feel, buddy?"

"She knew!" Jillian excitedly told me. "Bonnie figured out you were Chastity Wadsworth!"

"How?" I demanded. "I never told anyone."

"Never underestimate old ladies and their romance novels," my father philosophically said. "They…" He trailed off once he noticed the disapproving stares from every woman present, save Vance's daughters. "I think I'll shut up now."

My mom nodded. "That'd be a wise move, William."

"Did Samantha work for Semzar Pharmaceuticals?" Jillian suddenly asked.

I nodded. "Yes. Why?"

Jillian handed me another wad of dusty papers and yellowed clippings. She tapped one of the papers.

"She collected articles about Samantha, too. Look. Here's one stating that Semzar's amazing sales team had landed a contract worth millions of dollars. There's Samantha's name. Was she a sales rep?"

"She was," I confirmed, "and a darn good one at that. Sam could sell ice cubes to an Eskimo."

"She was mentioned by name a few times. Looks like Bonnie collected anything that mentioned her, too. It looks like she was an avid fan of both of you."

"Look at this," Tori said, holding a dusty piece of lined paper. "Looks like this was torn from a notepad. There's a hand-written note here addressed to Abigail. Let's see. She says that she has reviewed the offer and has to decline.

She cannot understand why her own flesh and blood aren't trying to make their own way in the world. Why do they have to keep coming after her and her winery? She also says that it'll be a cold day in hell before she'll ever see another label besides her own on one of her bottles."

"She loved her winery," Jillian said. "She told me that the time she invited me in for tea."

"When was this?" Tori asked.

"Years ago."

"The last thing she said was that she had to take steps to make sure the winery ended up in responsible hands and that she already had two worthy recipients in mind."

"She couldn't have chosen a better pair," my mother said in a quiet voice.

I took Jillian's hand in my own. I looked down at the corgis, who were snoozing by the fire. I glanced around the room at my family and friends. I reached for my glass of juice and held it up.

"I couldn't agree more. Here's to Aunt Bonnie and her fantastically awesome winery that everyone seems to love."

We clinked glasses.

"Hear, hear!" Tori cried. "I wish everyone a Merry Christmas!"

"And a Happy New Year," Jillian added.

"And a pocket full of money," I grinned.

"And a cooler full of beer," Vance finished.

Tori slugged him on the arm.

Zack and the corgis will be back right away in the
Case of the Pilfered Pooches
Dogs are missing! Chocolate Labs, cocker spaniels,
and even a German Shepherd have fallen victim to a
notorious dognapper, and the small-town citizens are
determined to take whatever means necessary to protect
their beloved pets. Now Zack, Sherlock and Watson
have been asked to look into the case. Can this favorite
canine duo sniff out the culprit and prevent panic from
spreading in Pomme Valley?
**Don't miss it! Subscribe to Jeff's newsletter and
receive news of all that's new with this exciting
series.**
Go to AuthorJMPoole.com to sign up.

* * *

The Corgi Case Files Series
Available in e-book and paperback

Case of the One-Eyed Tiger
Case of the Fleet-Footed Mummy
Case of the Holiday Hijinks
Case of the Pilfered Pooches
Case of the Muffin Murders
Case of the Chatty Roadrunner
Case of the Highland House Haunting
Case of the Ostentatious Otters
Case of the Dysfunctional Daredevils
Case of the Abandoned Bones
Case of the Great Cranberry Caper

AUTHOR'S NOTE

The plan for this particular book was to release it with the corresponding holiday. That's what I set out to do when I wrote *Case of the Fleet-Footed Mummy*. I thought it'd be cool to release a Halloween-themed story on, what else? Halloween!

It doesn't work so well when I miss my deadline. Dammit. So, I vowed I was going to repeat the experiment, only this time with Christmas. This book is the result, and I'm so very pleased to be able to say that I made it. True, Christmas is only a few days away, but I made it!

2017 is going to be one massive experiment for me. I've been trying for a while now to better organize myself and my time so that I can write more efficiently. Well, I've set a schedule and if I plan on keeping it, then I'm gonna have to buckle down. Here's the plan. Next up is a fantasy novel. I'm giving myself 2 months to write it. Then I hand it to my Posse. Then, while the book is being proofed/edited, I'll then commence work on a mystery. The mysteries, being easily half the size of the fantasies, should be able to be written in only a month. The book gets handed to my Posse and I'm off on the next, which will be another fantasy.

See the pattern? One fantasy (2 months), one mystery (one month), and then it repeats. Now, here's the scary part. If I can maintain that pace that'll mean I'll be able to pump out four fantasies and four mysteries in the same year.

That's the 2017 Plan. I don't know if I'll be able to make it but I'm planning on trying. I hope to keep my Posse busy this year.

Ok, I'm off to plot out some books. If I'm going to keep this schedule then it would help to have the books already plotted out. I've got some good ideas, including a prequel. Of sorts. Keep an eye on the blog. Whenever I get news I'll post it there.

Thank you very much for reading this far! I hope you enjoyed the book. I also would like to encourage you to leave a review if you enjoyed the book. Amazon, Barnes & Noble, or Kobo, it doesn't matter. Every review helps!

J.
December, 2016

Jeffrey M. Poole is a professional author living in sunny Phoenix, AZ, with his wife, Giliane and their Welsh Corgi, Kinsey.